Trial In Name Only

By Els Curtis

Cover art by H. A. England

ISBN: 9798608971952

This book is dedicated to Terry Pratchett, one of the biggest influence on my writing style, and a bad influence on my sense of humor. I never met you, but I wish I did.

Rest In Peace.

1948-2015

There are two stories that began with a plague of mice. This one doesn't have a musical instrument in it. As the story is told, first came the mice to New Hope, then the cats.[1] The infestation rivaled the plagues of Egypt. Mice swarmed in haylofts and silos, storerooms and pantries, pickle barrels and flour bins, in beds and shoes and bathtubs and undergarment drawers. They were bold enough to sit at the breakfast table, waiting to be served porridge and cream.

The mice convention arrived at a terrible time for the residents. New Hope was a fairly new settlement, the oldest home being a mere fifteen years. Despite the name, the town didn't come without problems. Facilities weren't as up-to-date as other countries, the natives refused to speak English no matter how loudly they shouted, and the children protested about leaving their friends behind.[2] And what was worse, a bad winter ate up the town's food reserves, resting all hope on the summer's crop. That's when the mice

---

[1] Some say the cats came first, but this makes no sense; those who tell it this way are the type who gets joke punchlines wrong.
[2] If they don't have to move because of religious intolerance, why do I?

came, like the tides during a full moon. The bumper crop couldn't be saved from the propagating mice that ate the grain right off the stalk. It wasn't even worth reaping.

As some spoke of abandoning the town, out of the forest appeared their salvation. At first, the heroes prowled in twos and threes, but each day their numbers grew. Kindles and clowders and glarings of blacks and whites, tabbies and torties, tails and tailless, short-haired and long-haired, an army of cats advanced on the town.

Storytellers are known to embellish. They had told how the cats marched with tails and heads held proudly, ready to set on the vermin like it was a mice-eating contest and the winner would get a bag of catnip. Anyone who has been around cats knows this isn't their way. More likely, they skulked, slunk, skittered, padded, and minced, pausing occasionally to wash a paw or their privates.

Their manner of entrance is neither here nor there; what mattered is that they arrived in droves, giving the farmers enough time to try their luck on a second crop for the year if the weather held.

Many saw the mice boom as merely bad luck which happened all the time. But who had ever heard of migrating cats? Such good luck had to be questioned. Some may have considered both groups of animals a coincidence, but others saw nothing but the supernatural.

One such individual, a reverend, heard this story while working in the city of Boston. By this time, the tale had grown more fantastical than reality, the proverbial fishing story. While most gossipers wouldn't turn their heads at such nonsense, the images of mice and cats twisted the reverend's noodle in a corkscrew.

The Reverend Michael Be-Steadfast Fear-God Kill-Sin Boggust, who wasn't known for spontaneity, promptly packed his bags, finished up what business he had in Massachusetts, and set off to follow what others laughed off as a tall-tale. In his wake strode his apprentice, a lad of eighteen who understood they went where the Lord wanted them to go.[3]

It was late September when the two arrived in New Hope, marching out of the woods like the cats glorified in the tales.[4] The reverend portrayed an imposing figure in his Puritan uniform that consisted of black, shades of black and a little bit of gray for variety. Between his wardrobe, pasty complexion and basement-black hair, there wasn't a speck of color save for his gold buckles and green eyes so dull they could have been rocks. With a tall, thin frame, he looked like a coat rack from behind. He walked with power and purpose, and wore piety like a wealthy man would rich, velvet raiment.

His apprentice sported a similar costume, but, to the reverend's consternation, he couldn't imitate that sanctimonious demeanor with his ruddy complexion and round face. In this case, the old adage wasn't true; clothing doth not maketh the man.

His entrance into New Hope was met with stares, not from the people, but from the cats. They peered at

---

[3] At least, where the reverend told him where the Lord wanted them to go. As long as the tithe was good…

[4] Except they refrained from licking themselves.

him with unabashed interest as if the two men were a small, monochromatic parade. The humans hardly noticed;[5] traveling ministers were common enough, preaching where they could for a small tithe and looking for an area to settle down. Some even saw this as a sign for good things to come[6] since the mice had driven away most traders and merchants.

Reverend Michael's first impression of the town went beyond his expectation. His cold gaze took in all the cats which numbered more than the people. He saw guilt and sin hidden behind masks of everyday life. There were signs everywhere of how far the people had fallen: a man, passed out in the streets, smelling of spirits, two women shouting at each other over a fence, a child playing in the dirt with corn husk dolls who was too old for such childishness, and a snaggle-toothed, black cat sitting nearby that looked as if God shoved its DNA into a blender.

Indeed, the reverend arrived just in the nick of time to save the town from the evils they allowed to ooze through the cracks and contaminate their souls. But he wasn't looking for just any everyday sin. He wasn't an ordinary preacher.

Reverend Michael Be-Steadfast Fear-God Kill-Sin Boggust was a witch-hunter.

His appearance began the third plague of New Hope: the plague of witches.

---

[5] Although, a few took note of the odd behavior in the cats. Where the attention of felines lie, a person can know, that is where the plot is.

[6] Ha ha ha. Oh, you.

*   *   *

The girl who sat in the dust and played with cornhusk dolls was called Constance.[7] She was thirteen, an age most girls gave up such silly things for other silly things like clothing and boys. But she wasn't like other girls. She loved her dolls; they understood her when nobody else did. Few could remember Constance's face since she preferred to hide behind a curtain of straight, mousy hair, and it was surprising to hear her voice since she spoke little.

The black cat belonged to Constance, but only in the way that certain people also belong to cats. His fur lacked any luster or smoothness and was as soft as a toilet brush. He had a fierce, wild appearance and lived up to it except in the presence of a chosen few. The cat was an open book on whether he preferred a person or not, a book that either purred like a racecar or used every weapon in a cat's arsenal. He smelled bad, and every day it was a different scent of awfulness. He was given the name of Lucifer by Constance's uncle, half-joking.[8]

Because the town cats took notice of the reverend, so did Constance, Lucifer, and the cornhusk dolls. Glancing up every few seconds, the girl hardly let the interruptions pause her imaginary game. She did not like looking into eyes; she let Lucifer and her dolls peer into the windows of her soul to help her

---

[7] She was called Constance because most people back then had unusually long names, and for the sake of brevity, it was best to shorten them.

[8] Half in earnest. One could never tell with cats.

understand the world. In those quick seconds, she had memorized the reverend's face, learning and remembering more than people gave her credit.

In the days to come, she learned more of the stranger from the whispers from her aunt, uncle, and neighbors, putting a name to the tall, scarecrow of a man. The information she soaked up had no significance to her, nor did she understand the profession of witch-hunter; it was just something that she knew.

She never forgot a name or a face.

*   *   *

Reverend Michael saw a project in the town, one that a large city like Boston couldn't give him. For one thing, it was like a painted canvas that needed some turpentine to wipe it clean before he could create something worth seeing. For another, there seemed to be no other witch-hunters to earn the glory for the Lord.

Before he could begin the Lord's work, there was the business of fussing over red tape. Once he and his apprentice had secured lodgings at the local inn, he drafted letters to the local leaders and ministers, informing them of his intent to hunt. Strangely enough, when a witch-hunter offers his service to weed out the wicked, men with power tend to stick their noses in where they're not wanted.[9] While it slowed the process, it was best to give them a head's up before heads rolled.

---

[9] It was not their business if he wanted to hang a few witches.

Diplomatically, he always ended each letter with a hint that the Lord would appreciate a tithe for the cause. Words were the foremost weapons in his arsenal.[10]

The sons of the innkeeper willingly delivered most of the letters, only one was entrusted to the apprentice with strict guidance not to return unless he carried a reply. That note was to the magistrate, who was the highest authority in the community. By the end of the day, the apprentice returned with a document stating that Reverend Michael was welcomed to perform his service within the township of New Hope.

The next day, he paid a visit to the local jail, which would become his base of operations. He was shocked at how shamefully inadequate the building was; the once cabin, transformed into a jail, had only one room with a single cell with a broken lock and no space for interrogating. How could he do his work without an interrogation room? Where would he torture confessions out of witches?

Even the jailor, who dozed in a tilted chair, was as much of a disappointment.

Used to the facilities of Boston where one could interrogate a witch in one room, torture in another, put them on trial in a third and lock them up somewhere cold and dank, New Hope was a far reach from ideal.

"You there. What is your name?"

"Eh?"

---

[10] They cut, they sting, they bite and wound. Some people never heal from such arms. The perfect weapon for a pacifist.

8

"Your name?" The reverend spoke deeper and clearer, showing his authority.

"Phinchas Partridge."

"Get up and straighten yourself out. Tuck in that shirt."

As if a drill sergeant was yelling at him, Phinchas did as he was told, dusting off his pants.

"This jailhouse is a disgrace, not fit for the work of God."

"I didn't think He'd be here."

"God is everywhere that idleness is not welcomed. And since He is to use this building for His purpose, it must be refurbished at once."

"Now? But it's empty."

"Is it always empty?"

"Mostly, except for the days Gilly drinks too much. Or when he drinks too little."[11]

"With a broken lock?"

"He knows to stay inside until he can properly behave."

The reverend sighed. He had been used to grander things in Boston, respect being the minimum requirement.

Leaving the training of Phinchas to his apprentice, Reverend Michael took over the single table and chair, ignoring the dust, cobwebs and mouse excrement. On this table, he placed a box of fine, lacquered oak, positioned so that the square of sunshine from the single window fell on it. He opened it with a relaxing exhale.

Inside lay several instruments on black velvet;

---

[11] Those were the worst days.

metal points and blades, teeth and ragged edges scrubbed shiny clean of skin, hair, and blood from the last witch.[12] He stroked his favorite, a pair of tweezers. Harmless in appearance when compared to its brothers, they caused far more pain when employed to pull out confessions from sinful mouths. He called them "The Wrath of God."

His chosen methods of torture differed than that of other witch-hunters. Where most preferred ostentatious machines that stretched limbs and whipped heads around, he preferred more subtle techniques. Small and simple things gave him a refined touch.

His Puritan parents had given him an unusual name, as was their right[13] with the hope that his incredibly long name would give him guidance in the future. And it had; he had followed the path to God, studying to be, not just any reverend, but a sacred witch-hunter. One of his given names particularly inspired his chosen profession: Fear-God. He had put the fear of God in many a malicious witch who dared persecute the innocent. He had done so in Boston, Hartford, Fairfield, and many other new colony cities. And he would do so here in New Hope.

But first, he needed to find them.

---

[12] A strange woman who had preached endlessly on the benefits of ritual hand-washing, claiming that it destroyed harmful creatures that were so small, they were invisible. What will these devil-worshippers think of next?

[13] Giving a baby an embarrassing name is the only legal form of child abuse, which, in turn, creates a bitter adult whose only release from this label is to procreate and assign an even more heinous name to their offspring. It's a vicious cycle.

*   *   *

On the morn, Reverend Michael explored the town, taking in the sights and sounds of the people, getting to know the thoroughfare and buildings. He discovered, through his apprentice, that New Hope was a hodge-podge of Puritans, Jews, Quakers, Catholics, and a smattering of different Protestant religions, all finding the shores of America a safe-haven from intolerance and a place of opportunity. The mixture of religions, in itself, concerned him. Being raised Puritan, he had been taught to distrust Catholics. But, his parents ingrained in him the valuable lesson that God required him to forgive everyone, even Catholics.[14]

With each new face that he inspected, he scrutinized for the tell-tale signs of guilt, the lowering of eyes, slumped shoulders, and sketchy glances. He knew that gossip—a lesser evil that worked to his advantage—would spread that a witch-hunter had arrived. He made sure Phinchas would talk by forbidding the jailor from uttering a word.

To his disappointment, his reputation hadn't preceded him; the townsfolk peered at him with unabashed curiosity and gave him friendly nods and waves. The children didn't become somber and wary in his presence, but laughed and gamboled as they continued their games. One man even had the audacity to converse about the weather.

And not a single guilty face among them.

---

[14] Nobody's perfect.

He was on the verge of retreating back to the inn with another hunting strategy when he spotted her. The crone sat in a rocking chair on her porch, wrapped tightly in a blanket despite the Indian summer. She was as crooked as a tree with hair the color of ash. Three cats sat on her lap, one slung around her shoulders like a scarf, four at her feet, and dozens stalking or sunbathing around her house. And the most prominent characteristic: a dark, splotchy spot on her cheek, a devil's mark.

Plus, she owned a broom. He could see it plain as day leaning against the doorframe. It was as if she wanted to be caught.

Damning evidence if he ever saw it.

*   *   *

While many eyes had seen the witch-hunter during his stroll, nobody was around to witness the first ever arrest for witch-craft in the province, except for young Constance, who sat in a patch of weeds, drawing designs in the dirt with a stick. Lucifer saw, but nobody counted him.[15]

The woman whom the witch-hunter apprentice escorted to the shabby jailhouse was Faithful Goodman, an elderly woman of over seventy years, along with two cats she had clutched to her bosom and wouldn't let go. She had been a widow these last eighteen years, and with no family nearby, had been watched over by her neighbors and Christian charity.

---

[15] The cat, not the other one. Although nobody can be sure he didn't see.

A saint to the local cats, she had welcomed the legions of felines, feeding them as best she could when the mouse population dropped substantially.

Faithful liked cats more than children, but she still left a section of her heart for the little dears as long as they were kind to animals and her cats liked them.[16] Addled and forgetful, she often spoke about Constance to others not unkindly but not with kid-gloves, forgetting to whisper when referring to "That girl that's touched in the head" and sometimes even calling her a "lunatic."[17]

Words never bothered Constance, and she was ignorant of the slight mistreatment. But even with this small rudeness, Faithful was still kind to Constance, giving compliments about the girl's hair when it was brushed or giving her biscuits.

The cat, on the other hand, was another matter. Faithful's love of cats ended at Lucifer. She hardly considered the half-wild feline to be part of the species. It would have been easier to believe that Lucifer's parentage was closer to the wolverine

---

[16] Woe until the child who offends a pet of Goody Faithful. She held the opinion of cats above that of most.

[17] Which was quite common back then. Anyone who appeared different, acted different, had different thoughts or stood out in any way was considered mad, like the hysterical, the lazy, those with over active minds, those with under active minds, those whose parents were cousins, drug users, religious enthusiast, political enthusiast, sexual enthusiasts, asthmatics, those with women troubles, those who are jealous, the suppressed, the superstitious the greedy, the bereaved, the seduced, the seducers, the self-abused, the abusers, the feeble, the deranged, and those who see witches where there are no witches to be seen.

family or at least something that could bring down a deer.

As Faithful and the cats entered the jailhouse, she had no idea for what reason she had been summoned. Even if she understood the situation and cried for help, the only witnesses, Constance and Lucifer, weren't the kind that could tell someone. They were only what they could be, witnesses of the event of the first witch arrest in New Hope.

*   *   *

Reverend Michael lit a single candle and placed it on the wobbly table. He had also blacked out the window to set the mood in anticipation for his first unaided witch interrogation. Back in Boston, Fairfield, and everywhere else he practiced the fine arts of witch-hunting, he had always been accompanied by other priests and religious ministers who also geared to do the Lord's business. But here, he was alone in this war against evil. Finally, this was his test.

As his apprentice marched the elderly witch in, her familiars yowled their irritation. Just like the demons they were, they had no respect for anyone.

"Goody Goodman, I am Reverend Michael Be-Steadfast Fear-God Kill-Sin Boggust," he spoke. With his deep somber voice, he felt the atmosphere was enough to cow the woman.

"Good name," the woman complimented. "You can tell by how much repentance it reminds one to do."

"I bet it does." The reverend smiled.

"Of course, being name Faithful, I understand being a reminder to follow the Lord."

Oh, she is good, the reverend thought. If he didn't know better, he may have thought of Faithful as a sweet, old lady. "Judgement Day has come for you. You're hereby accused—"

"Reverend, shouldn't we have a prayer first?" Faithful held out her hand.

"No!... I mean…Yes, we can pray," Reverend Michael sputtered. His eyes strayed to his apprentice who sat in the room with parchment, quill, and inkpot, recording the reverend's words for future clergymen to judge. He reluctantly clasped the woman's hand before raising his voice to heaven.

"O Lord, who art in heaven, we thank thee for thy grace and wisdom, for thy mercy and judgement. Bless us, O Lord, that we may repent of our sins. Forgive us, that we may be forgiven." His once peaceful voice rose in tempo, condemning and justified. "And help us, O Lord, that we may find every demon-spawned witch before they turn the head of thy flock. Save us from their wicked intents and powers, that they may be cast into the burning pits. Amen."

"Amen," Faithful echoed reverently.

Releasing her hand, the reverend slammed his fist on the table. "I know you're a witch. Confess!"

The cats turned into a single dervish before pretending the loud noise didn't startle them by washing frantically.

"You don't have to yell," Faithful scolded, petting the felines. "Now, which what are you looking for?"

"No. A witch."

"Which what?"

"I'm looking for witches. WITCHES."

"There are ditches all over. It shouldn't be hard to find one."

"I'm a witch-hunter. I'm looking for a witch."

Faithful patted his hand consolingly. "I'm sure you'll find your niche. You're still young."

The reverend reached for The Wrath of God, sure that Faithful was mocking him, but withdrew, refusing to be baited. There would be time later to use the tweezers. "I know what you are. I've seen the signs. Your familiars gave you away."

"What are you familiar with?"

"Your cats," the witch-hunter seethed.

"Ah, I do apologize. I'm sorry if my sweeties have clawed your furniture or did their business in your garden. I'll speak to them."

"Ah-ha, so you admit that you talk to your cats—er, familiars."

"Of course I'm familiar with them. They's cats. Once you know them, it isn't hard to understand them. Watch Mittens here. See how her ears swivel around; that means—"

"I don't care what it means. You admit that you can talk to cats. You have a broom and a witch's mark. You are a witch."

"A mark? That can't be. My skin is as white as cream." Faithful rubbed her cheek as if she were twenty.

Reverend Michael produced a hand mirror for proof.

"Oh my. Has that been there this whole time?"

She licked her thumb and rubbed the spot away. "Must a'bin the stew."

The cats sniffed her thumb, hoping for a treat.

The reverend rubbed his face. "Confess, woman."

"I'm not Catholic," Faithful sniffed. "My sins are nobody's business but mine and the Lord's, thank you very much."

"Enough of your ramblings," Reverend Michael ordered, throwing up his hands in righteous anger. "Feigning ignorance won't save you. Give me names. Who are the other witches?"

A conspiring expression fell on Faithful. She looked around as if spies were in all the nooks and crannies, then covered the ears of one of her cats before leaning forward and whispering, "Edith Partridge."

"Edith Partridge?" Reverend Michael glanced at his apprentice to make sure the name was written down.

Faithful nodded. "Someone told Pastor Smith that it was I who stole the apple pie from Mrs. Hutchins' window last week. I didn't do it, but I know it was her who told him. She's a snitch if there ever was one."

Snitch. Witch. Same thing.

It wasn't common practice to allow a witch to go free, especially since she just as good as confessed. Normally, he would press for other names with the help of his lacquered box, but Faithful wasn't the most exemplar subject. She was small and wrinkled and would remind most of their grandmothers. The hearts of men were easily swayed by the frail and elderly, even if under that façade was a deviant. In the interest of New Hope, Goody Goodman would be set free.

"Your confession has pleased the Lord. You may leave," Reverend Michael acquiesced.

Faithful gathered her cats before tottering away, mumbling, "What a nice man."

As the apprentice finished writing down the interrogation, the reverend watched the backside of Faithful where two sets of narrow pupils glared at him. He would allow the old witch to go free, but there was one thing he knew for sure. Those two cats, as well as all the rest in town, would not be so lucky.

*   *   *

The next day, Reverend Michael sent his apprentice out to wrangle as many cats as he could. While most witch-hunters didn't bother with this rabble, Reverend Michael made it a priority to deal with familiars and demon-spawn at the beginning. Not only were they the eyes and ears for the evil one, he also detested their high and mighty attitudes. It was irritating being in a room with a creature who thought they were better than you.

The apprentice hated this part of the job. He wasn't specifically partial to cats; he had a love for all of God's creatures. It wasn't his fault that witch familiars tended to be on the feline side of the animal kingdom. According to the reverend, even if not all the cats were familiars, they were guilty by species association and would receive the same treatment.

It wasn't hard for the apprentice to find cats; they were as abundant as bed bugs in a one-star hotel. They appeared to be friendly, docile creatures until the second that the apprentice laid hands upon them, then they turned into devilish tornados of claws and fur. Scratched and wounded, the apprentice returned to his master at midday with only a single kitten in hand, a grey and white with one eye, three legs and a half of a tail, which had still given him quite a fight.

At the sight of Reverend Michael's disapproving glare, the apprentice explained how helpless he had been against the hordes of cats, playing to the reverend's sympathy by making his battle-wounds worse than they appeared. He didn't take in account that the reverend had no empathy.

"I'll forgive you your human weakness against the face of evil this once. But I expect you to strengthen your spirit tonight and try again in the morning," the reverend sniffed. "We have much to do. Let us begin the trial."

The witch-hunter strongly believed all of God's creations deserved a trial, even cats.[18] Most witch-hunters would just drown them right off, but Reverend Michael gave them a chance to defend themselves before drowning them.[19]

The apprentice, per habit, fetched quill, ink, and parchment to record the trial. This was also a task the apprentice despised. Back in Boston, he had recorded dozens of cat trials each day, and eventually, the tedious scribbling overshadowed the surrealism.

---

[18] It was part of his benevolent side.

[19] His mercy is unmeasurable.

Inside the jailhouse, under the same conditions as Goody Goodman's interrogation, they held the trial for the kitten.

The apprentice, for the sake of anyone who would read the transcripts, often gave the cats names so that anyone reading the records wouldn't think they interrogated the same cat over and over again.[20] Referring to his old Latin lessons, he gave the kitten the name "Tripod."

With the kitten sitting in a cage on the table, Reverend Michael began, waiting until the apprentice wrote down the location, date and details regarding this trial.

"You are accused of witchcraft. How do you plea?"

The apprentice was under obligations to record everything that could be interpreted as a response from the "accused," including silence.

"Let the record show," Reverend Michael said, "that the accused refuses to answer. Are you, in fact, a witch or a witch's familiar, sworn to serve the devil?"

Tripod settled down in the cage and closed its eyes, all of which were recorded.

"Let the record show that the accused refuses to answer again. The accused is now in contempt of court."[21]

Tripod meowed loudly. The apprentice recorded it.

---

[20] That would just be ridiculous.

[21] This happens a lot. Cats just prefer to remain in a state of contempt. It saves them time.

"Ah-ha, now you speak. Do you have any evidence to dispute the charges against you?"

Tripod licked its shoulder disdainfully.[22] That was also recorded.

"Let the record show that the accused has no evidence. The court takes the accused's silence as an admission of guilt."

By this time, the kitten had moved from cleaning its shoulder to washing beneath its tail, an obvious insult to the reverend. The apprentice wrote this down.

"By the power vested in me by the Almighty, on the charges of witchcraft and aiding and abetting a witch, I find you guilty. The sentence is death by drowning. May God have mercy on your soul." The reverend's words were as final as a judge's gavel and as sobering as an executioner's job.

The kitten yawned and turned its back on the court, ignoring the danger it was in. This did not go unnoticed by the apprentice, who tried to portray the kitten as brave, despite it being a sinful creature.[23]

"Deal with it," the reverend spoke to his apprentice before whisking out the door.

Now came the part that the apprentice really, really hated: Carrying out the sentence. When he decided to become a witch-hunter's apprentice, this had not been part of the job description, but he had little choice. It was either this or return home as a

---

[22] The apprentice often editorialized the cats' emotions. While most cats do not speak, they can be open books when they want to be.

[23] It's a cat. It had to be guilty of something.

failure in a simple apprenticeship.

Carrying the cage, he headed for the river nearly mile and a half away. In Boston, where he first joined up with Reverend Michael, he paid street boys or urchins to perform the dastardly deed of taking a sack of cats to the ocean, but the rare occasion that he had to do it himself, he hated it every time.[24]

As he made it to the bank of the river—listening to the mewing of Tripod the whole way—he recalled the other executions he performed. He felt guilty for taking those lives, even though the Lord had ordained their deaths. It was the Lord's will for him to throw this cage—the whole kitten and caboodle—into the river. It made him sick thinking about it. But he couldn't go against his duty, his calling. Look what happened to Jonah.[25]

As he raised the cage, ready to heave, he looked at Tripod, seeing the missing eye, the missing leg, and the missing half a tail; it had not had a good start on life. And now this. If he hadn't caught the kitten, some wild animal would kill it eventually as weak and malformed as it was.

Then the kitten mewed softly and reached through the bars of the cage to pat his hand as if to say, "I understand."

A minute later, the apprentice heaved the cage, aiming for a part of the river that had a rock sticking

---

[24] He had refused at first, telling Reverend Michael that the practice was barbaric and bias. "Only a witch would think so," the reverend replied. This argument was so persuasive, the apprentice had never complained ever again.

[25] The posterboy of cautionary tales from the Bible.

out where the cage bounced before plopping into deeper water. Taking off his shoes and stockings, he rolled up his trousers and waded out to retrieve the cage.

All the while, Tripod sat on the shore and watched with interested, having been released moments ago. It twitched its tail stump as the apprentice came ashore with a dripping, dented cage.

"I hope that's convincing," the apprentice said as Tripod inspected it. He waved a hand at the kitten. "Shoo. Get. We'll both be in trouble if the witch-hunter sees you."

The kitten mewed and rubbed up against his leg.

The young man pushed the kitten away with his foot. "Oh, you'll probably be dead soon anyway. Just do it in the forest, will you?"

Replacing his shoes and stockings, he marched toward New Hope, leaving the kitten to sunbathe on a boulder and expecting to never see it again.[26]

All the way back, the story of Jonah recited through his thoughts. What would God do to him for disobeying? Worse, what would Reverend Michael do? He thought about confessing the moment he saw his master, throwing himself to the mercy of God. Would it not be better to admit his guilt now instead of letting himself be found out?

However, he didn't have the chance to speak a word. At a glance of the apprentice's face, Reverend Michael sent him out again to capture more witch familiars, heedless of the dangers he was sending his young charge out into.

---

[26] No, this isn't foreshadowing or anything of the kind.

Less contrite, the apprentice did as he was told, but with only a quarter-hearted effort. He silently thanked they were nowhere near the ocean.

*   *   *

Displeased with his apprentice's lack of success, Reverend Michael did not send him out a second day to snatch up cats. Instead, he sent the young man to bring in Edith Partridge whom Goody Goodman had accused. The youth seemed keen to obey—or rather, not have to deal with more cats—and set off right away.

It wasn't long before the apprentice returned with a red handprint on his cheek and excuses a mile long. Apparently Edith Partridge wasn't just a big woman, but also had big ideas and opinions and a loud voice.[27] There was nothing an eighteen-year-old witch-hunter's apprentice could do to persuade her to come to the jailhouse.

With a heavy sigh directed toward the heavens, Reverend Michael sent the apprentice out again, this time accompanied by Phinchas Partridge, the jailor. The jailor was even more reluctant to retrieve his wife since the consequences were direr for him if they succeeded. He even volunteered to round up cats rather than bring in his wife. Not on account that she was accused as a witch,[28] but because at some point or another, he'd have to be alone with her.

---

[27] A dangerous combination.

[28] He already suspected such.

Reverend Michael heard them before they arrived back at the jailhouse, at least he heard Edith. Earlier he had sensed she was a difficult woman[29] and had retreated to the back of the jailhouse to give the woman time to cool down.

Apparently Edith had no cool-down period. The minute she was shown a seat in the darkened room, she complained and shouted to be released. The reverend would have normally given her time to sit and brew in her own sweat[30] but even he felt anxious, and he wasn't even the one she was yelling at.

As he stepped in with shadowed calmness, he dismissed the sweating Phinchas who was grateful to get out of his wife's line of sight.

There was barely room for the reverend, the apprentice, and the robust woman, who had finally closed her mouth so she could glare better; her overlarge belly was due to either too much time in the kitchen or the bedroom. Reverend Michael hoped the former; it wouldn't reflect well on his profession to probe[31] a woman with child.

"Whatever you want, do it quick." The woman's tone and crossed arms shouted her distaste. "I have nine boys between the ages of two an' sixteen who're all hell-bent on killin' themselves or each other when I'm not watchin'."

"Goody Partridge, you are accused of performing witchcraft. How do you plead?"

"What?"

---

[29] Did anyone say "understatement"?

[30] Only an hour or two.

[31] And by "probe," he means "torture."

The reverend wondered if everyone of New Hope suffered an ailment of the ear. He spoke louder and slower. "You…have…been...accus—"

"I heard you the first time. I'm just stunned. Does this have anythin' to do with Faithful an' the pie? You can't believe a word that woman says; she's taken leave of her senses."

"This goes beyond stealing pies, Madam. Answer the question."

"I've never heard such a ridiculous declaration."

Shakespeare said it best, "The lady doth protest too much."[32]

"I repeat. Are you a witch?"

"No, I ain't."

At first, the conversation felt akin to the one he had with Faithful. The elderly woman's words had struck a discordant note and prevented the witch-hunter from hitting his stride. However, with the pronounced denial, comfort washed over him. When truth was rejected, that's where he could do his work.

"Do you know why I'm here?"

"Askin' me dumb questions, that's what."

"No, woman, I'm on the Lord's business. Are you a God-fearing woman?" He smiled as he invoked one of his names.[33]

"I go to church every Sunday an' teach my children from the Bible."

"An intelligent answer from a deceitful mouth.

---

[32] Not that the reverend put much stock in Shakespeare and his plays. With all those witches and ghosts, he was sure the playwright dipped his quill in the dark arts himself.

[33] They don't call him Reverend Michael Be-Steadfast Fear-God Kill-Sin Boggust for nuthin'.

You want me to think because you attend church and know the Bible that you're righteous, but I cannot be deceived. I know who you are. I've broken witches cleverer than you. Answer truthfully; are you a witch?"

"You're mad," Edith declared, standing. "I won't abide this. I'm leavin'."

With a gesture from his master, the apprentice stopped writing and persuaded the woman to sit back down with firm hands. However, it was like pushing on a mule; the boy had to throw his entire weight into his urging.

"Get your hands off me. When my husband find out how you've been treatin' me, you'll get it," Edith threated. She raised her voice. "Phinchas. Phinchas. Get in here."

Either the man didn't heed the call of his wife or he had escaped beyond the reach of her influence, which meant he fled out of self-preservation.

During this, the witch-hunter turned his back on the accused, fondling his lacquered box. "My parents gave me many names. One of those names is Kill-Sin. They died when I was but a lad. I believe they wanted me to call the sinful back to Him. It's not too late for you. All you need to do is confess and renounce your evil ways."

"Your threats may frighten them Boston girls, but that won't work on me. I've given birth nine times, three of 'em breach, an' the next day, I cooked meals an' hauled firewood."

Her voice was like a challenge. Reverend Michael opened the box, letting his hand hover over the iron instruments. He lingered at The Wrath of

God but changed his mind. Instead, he chose a long needle that was specifically designed to check for burned off or removed witch marks;[34] if the needle penetrated and blood wasn't drawn, this was evidence of witchery.[35]

And even if this test failed, it wasn't definite proof. The revered had many tests; one was bound to prove eventual guilt.[36]

When the reverend turned with the needle in hand, Edith let out a squeal of shock that belied her earlier bravado. She leaned back in her chair so dramatically, it threatened to tip. She nearly broke the third commandment.[37]

"Your sins must be killed. Now, do I need to ask the question again?" the witch-hunter inquired, his voice as smooth as a newly molted snake.

Edith licked her lips, her eyes locked on the needle. "If I answer, are you gonna stick me with that thing?"

She may not have been the smartest woman, but the reverend could tell that she finally discerned whom she was dealing with. "Depends," he answered cryptically. "If you speak the truth, you have no fear. God does not punish the honest."

In this position, many would question whether

---

[34] Or could be poked in any place, really.

[35] Unknown to those being poked (and in some cases, the poker), the makers of such needles actually designed the instrument to not draw blood whether it be used on a witch or non-witch. It's the results that matters.

[36] It's persistence that wins the day.

[37] And to be honest, the fifth and perhaps a few others that weren't numbered.

Reverend Michael and God were on the same page. More likely, they weren't even in the same genre. But God wasn't the one in the room holding something sharp.

"Yes, I do believe I may be a witch," Edith said slowly.

Reverend Michael put the needle down, disappointed and satisfied at the same time. He was content that the Lord's work was progressing, but he had expected—almost hoped—that the interrogation would last longer. "For the record, give details of your sins. What have you done in your service as a witch to the devil?"

"Witchy stuff. You know, catchin' toads, makin' potions, runnin' around skyclad at midnight. That kind of thing."

"Have you afflicted people with your dark arts?"

"Yeah, loads.

"Whom?"

"What for? I confessed as you wanted. Can I go now?"

"Madam, I don't think you realize the severity of your situation. You're dangerously close to losing your soul. The punishment for witchcraft is death by hanging."

Whatever courage remained after the needle incident melted away. "No, no. Please, have mercy. I was lyin'."

"Yes, a servant of the devil would be quick to lie, especially when it comes to saving their life."

"No, I ain't really a witch. I was sayin' that so you wouldn't stick that thing in me. Please, don't do this. I'm a mother. My babies need me."

The witch-hunter smiled. This was more like it; this is what he expected. This was respect. Not as satisfying as The Wrath of God, but it would do. "God is not without mercy," he placated. "Turn from the Devil and renounce your evil ways."

"An' I'll live?"

"If you're contrite, and it be God's will."[38]

"I am. I renounce being a witch. I never liked it anyway. It's a horrible, thankless job. The hours I spent cleanin' my cauldron and castin' spells. An' does that husband of mine watch the children when I have to ride my broom? No, never lifts a finger. Why, there was one time—"

The reverend cleared his throat. "Yes, that's good to declare your intentions, but the Lord needs more. You must prove that you're repentant."

"How? I already go to church an' read the Bible. Should I do it twice as much?"

"Flippancy isn't contrite. You can show your penitence by naming your fellow witches."

"But I don't know any witches."

"The Devil is a tricky one; he kept you and the other witches separated, but you must know of at least one. Perhaps you saw her or him at one of your witches' Sabbats."

"I don't know," Edith said uncertainly. "It's one thing for me to say I'm a witch, but to accuse someone else…that wouldn't be Christian. No, I'm sure there's no other witches in Ne—"

Reverend Michael picked up the needle again.

"Ida Vassal an' Temperance Firman. I saw them

---

[38] Or the reverend's. Either way.

at Sabbat. An' Thou-Will-Be-Done Matson an' Clarence Porter. Faithful Goodman, she's a great witch. Goody Stanford, Benevoline Cribb, Olivia Crawson, they's all witches. An' I saw Thelma Vermain cursin' at cows on a Sunday."[39]

She babbled so quickly, the apprentice had trouble scribbling.

"You're penance has been accepted, that is, if these names check out."

"You're gonna talk to them?"

"Of course. I am called by God to hunt down the servants of evil. It would be negligent of me to allow these witches to continue their dark arts."

Edith looked ill.

"And, of course, I'll have to talk to your children."

"Why?" Edith glared.

The reverend paced as if lecturing a class. "It stands to reason that your children may be influenced by your witchcraft. I have, of course, interviewed your husband, and he was lucky enough to have kept himself clean of your power. My apprentice will bring in your...how many was it...nine children? They'll be questioned and punished accordingly. In the meantime, you are hereby sentenced to either three weeks in prison or three days in the stocks."

"But I thought givin' you names would absolve me of my sins."

"In the eyes of God, but the laws of man still need to be satisfied."

---

[39] This last one is the most likely to be true. It's hard not to curse at a cow, even on a Sunday.

Edith sighed in defeat, shifting her belly. "I'd prefer the prison over the stocks; don't want the neighbors to see me. An' I'll get to see what my husband does around here all day."

"Fine, fine. My apprentice will escort you."

As Edith waddled out of the interrogation room and into the single cell—still with a broken lock—Reverend Michael muttered, "Faithful was right. She is a snitch."[40]

*   *   *

New Hope was a town that was off the beaten path, only visited by families of residents and small-time merchants, traders, and peddlers. Due to this, they were often left alone to their own devices when it came to governing themselves, as long as they paid their taxes. And the town preferred it that way.

The town was small enough that they needed only one man to act as both mayor and magistrate, a man by the name of Abraham Hiddlesby. Among the farmers, ranchers and tradesmen of the town, he was a man who knew how to delegate to a crowd of nay-sayers, conduct a meeting without all the twaddle, and knew exactly when to be fair and when to be unfair to make it fair for everyone.

When Reverend Michael's letter of introduction crossed his desk, gooseflesh rose on Mr. Hiddlesby's

---

[40] Some might question the authenticity of the use of the word "snitch." Historically, it cannot be traced far enough back to be used in this context. For those etymologists scrutinizing this tale, just substitute a more historically acceptable word, one that rhymes with "snitch" and "witch."

arms. His grandfather was a merchant, and when he returned from travels from foreign parts, he would bring home stories. Some of them were filled with wonder and adventure, funny and wise. But some were frightening. And not the way monsters and ghosts are scary, because those stories aren't real or are too far away to reach home. These stories involved people with power such as the Spanish Inquisition.

At first, Mr. Hiddlesby intended to write back to the witch-hunter to ask him to move on. Traveling ministers weren't uncommon, even in a remote place like New Hope. Often times they would preach at one church or another for a few weeks, gather whatever tithes the congregation would give, then move on. Reverend Michael was the first one who specialized in witch-hunting.

But before Mr. Hiddlesby set ink to parchment, he recalled those stories he heard as a boy. Growing up in England and not being Catholic, he had little fear of the Spanish Inquisition, but there was still a childish dread of what they did to heretics and witches that had given him nightmares; those memories lingered even as he moved to the new colonies as an adult.

He had also heard news from a cousin living in Boston of the witch-hunting going on there, similar to what he heard about the Spanish Inquisition. He wondered if he turned away this witch-hunter, would the man return and report back to Boston? Would he think there was something to hide? Would he think that the magistrate had secrets if he was turned away?

Fear won over, and he allowed Reverend Michael to officiate his business in the jailhouse, hoping that the witch-hunter would merely make a few harmless inquiries before collecting a tithe and moving on. Just to be safe, he wrote to his cousin, inquiring about this particular witch-hunter.

Days later, Mr. Hiddlesby's desk was riddled with angry letters and complaints, telling of beloved pet cats being chased around, the rough treatment of elderly women, and the imprisonment of the whole Partridge family, including the youngest of two years. The final shoe dropped when word that Edith Partridge had her baby in jail.[41]

This was an outrage, an injustice. The reverend had gone too far. While Reverend Michael had jurisdiction in God's law, Mr. Hiddlesby was the magistrate in this part of the country. He had to step in.

Yet Mr. Hiddlesby wasn't the sort to jump into a problem on the word of many; he needed to see things for himself. Putting on his coat and hat, he walked down to the jailhouse. Where once a quiet, peaceful building stood now had been turned into a madhouse of screaming and climbing savages that was the Partridges, and in the middle of it all sat Goody Partridge, nursing the newborn.

"If I knowed he were gonna put all of us in here, I'd have asked for the stocks," Edith grumbled after telling her side of the story. "It's bad enough that my reputation is the subject of all gossip, but I shouldn't have to be locked up with my children."

---

[41] Turns out she wasn't just fat.

Mr. Hiddlesby was glad she hadn't been put in the stocks. The last thing he needed was for gossip to spread about a woman from New Hope giving birth like a yoked oxen.

"I assure you, Goody Partridge, I'll sort things out with Reverend Michael," Mr. Hiddlesby assuaged. "The idea of passing judgement on you for the crime of witchcraft. Ridiculous."[42]

"You see that you do," Edith scolded as she would her children. "An' when you see that no-good husband of mine, bring him in here. This jailhouse is an absolute mess. If he's gettin' all them wages, he should be pulling more of his weight around. An' would it kill him to get some more candles. I swear, I could…"

Mr. Hiddlesby nodded mechanically as he backed up slowly, smiling in an assuring way.

"An' tell that Faithful Goodman that I knowed what she did. I'm gonna get her back."

Stepping out of the jailhouse, the magistrate noticed Mr. Partridge hugging the wall just outside the door, pretending to be part of the structure. He felt sorry for the poor man with a wife like that and ten children. It almost kept him silent about the man's presence.

Almost.

"I've found your husband, Goody Partridge," Mr. Hiddlesby announced, shoving the cowering man,

---

[42] It wasn't that she was found guilty of committing witchcraft that was ridiculous—Mr. Hiddlesby always knew Edith was capable of any crime she decided to execute—it was that the judgement was pronounced without his say so.

throwing him to the proverbial lion.

Having the rumors confirmed, the magistrate went directly to his office where he pondered over what to do. He had no peers, no advisors, and had no time to write to his cousin for guidance. At times, he had organized town meetings to take a consensus of what the town thought. Perhaps, this would be one of those times, although he would keep the forum closed to only those invited.

Drafting a list, Mr. Hiddlesby included all men of influence and affluence, religious leaders, business owners, and those that had proven natural-born leaders during times of strife. No doubt some would bring their wives, which he counted on. Despite their sex, women could provide sound advice.[43]

And above all, the witch-hunter was not to know anything about the meeting.

*   *   *

While most children were born without the good sense to keep their curiosity in check, Constance had little interest in the newcomer, yet she had made the connection that this stranger was the epicenter of the hustle and bustle that was stirring up the town and making her aunt and uncle so nervous. The adults talked in her presence, thinking she wouldn't comprehend. In reality, she understood everything; it just meant nothing to her. Their tones, on the other hand, upset her.

She had seen old Goody Goodman being taken in

---

[43] In that day and age, this was considered a compliment.

and heard about Edith Partridge being thrown in jail. She had even investigated since she liked to play around the jailhouse where there was a gopher burrow there that Lucifer liked to watch. But whenever she heard the newborn baby crying, she would cover her ears, hating how the sound grated on her skin, sliding up and down her nerves like a bow across an out-of-tune violin. She stopped going there after that, which upset her even more.

And then her aunt and uncle spoke to her about going to a town meeting. They had been invited since her uncle was the preacher of a small Presbyterian church. Constance was glad they told her in advance; she didn't like having her routine disturbed on short notice. Normally, either her aunt or uncle would remain at home at all times since Constance made a fuss if they both left without her. After all, her parents had left her alone one day, and they didn't come back.

On the day of the town meeting, her aunt reminded her.

"Constance, honey, do you understand? We're going to Mr. Hiddlesby's."

Constance looked out the window, avoiding her aunt's eyes. She hated finding words of her own; they never lined up in her mind how she wanted. So she used borrowed words. "'For whither thou goest, I will go; and where thou lodgest, I will lodge: thy people shall be my people, and thy God my God.'"

She could hear the smile in her aunt's voice. "That's from the Book of Ruth, right Constance?"

Her aunt touched her hair, and Constance shied away with a shrug. She was slowly getting used to the contact, but it bothered her. She was happy for the compliment, giving her best smile which was a twitch at the corner of her mouth. After all, she had most of the Bible memorized, having remembered nearly everything spoken to her, including when her parents read from the scriptures. It made her comfortable to be able to talk with the words of God.

"Let's go."

Constance took her aunt's hand on one side, her uncle's on the other, the only human contact she liked. It didn't bother her that she was beyond the age where most children refrained from this act with their parents; it made her feel safe, secure, as if nothing bad would happen.

Unfortunately, the cat would have to stay. Before leaving, she told the creature, "Get thee hence, Lucifer." It wasn't an exact quote, but the cat understood and wasn't offended, taking a nap on the porch until his companion returned.

*   *   *

The day of the town meeting, Mr. Hiddlesby received a letter from his cousin in Boston about Reverend Michael. Just as his hair follicles had warned him, it turned out that Reverend Michael Be-Steadfast Kill-Sin Fear-God Boggust wasn't just a zealous supporter of the witch-trials in the theocracy of Boston's leaders; he also saw witches everywhere he went: Hartford, Fairfield, and several other cities. He didn't just take his job seriously, he breathed it like a fish in water. If he pointed in a crowd, suddenly there was a witch. It was as if witches threw themselves in his path.

One could say that his finger made witches appear out of thin air.

But in those other cities, he had experienced, established men, preachers and ministers, who had the final decision. He had never been the witch-hunter in charge.

There was no such barrier in New Hope. Reverend Michael could work unchecked without peers to staunch the flow of fanatical finger-pointing. No, that wouldn't do. Mr. Hiddlesby had to do something about that. After all, he couldn't have rogue witch-hunters accusing people willy-nilly.

The town meeting took place in Thou-Will-Be-Done Matson's barn. Thou-Will was gracious to keep the barn mostly clear for such occasions like dances, meetings, and family reunions; it was the largest structure close to the town. An added bonus was that he was meticulous in cleaning more than most farmers, moving the animals to pasture for the time, mucking it out, and spreading fresh straw. Since he had been busy working himself dog-tired from coaxing a second, late crop from the soil, it was surprising he made it to the meeting.

Some brought along chairs while most sat on hay bales or stood. A few cats prowled the outskirts of the crowd, silent and irritated that their home had been infested by humans. At least, thanks to the felines, the mice had been cleared out.

Like always, they began the meeting with a prayer after the ministers had figured out which denomination hadn't been represented recently before Mr. Hiddlesby stood on Thou-Will's wagon box. He noticed that despite limiting the amount of invitations, there were more citizens gathered than expected. At least, it was devoid of children and youth save for the Sanderson girl, who acted like a child despite being on the cusp of womanhood, but she was no bother, never disturbing adults except to recite a scripture here and there, which was her way.

"Gentlemen...and ladies...I have heard your concerns regarding Reverend Michael. It seems he has taken more liberties than is within his power. However, my biggest worry is the reputation of our town. New Hope has always been centered on family values and morals found in the good book, and I am wary of what this man will say on his travels if we treat him less than civilly. As you know, I have a cousin in Boston, and he reports that this witch-hunter is not without reputation."

This announcement caused a stir; status was all New Hope had to bring in any new blood. Settlers were coming by the boatload, and there were plenty of areas for them to find a home.

"I heard he's taking names," Thomas Biddle, a rich merchant, shouted from the back. "What's he taking names for?"

"Does he think there are actually witches in New Hope?" one woman asked.

"That apprentice of his was chasin' cats by our barn last night. How can decent folk live in peace with boys chasin' cats all over?" another protested.

Mr. Hiddlesby raised his hands, hoping to quell all comments as they bombarded him. "I understand that his methods are...strange at the least, and maybe harsh, but what would it look to the rest of the world if we stopped a witch-hunter from doing his job. I have seen that he has crossed lines he shouldn't, but I would like to deal with this calmly and logically. Witches are being found in Boston and Fairfield, and if they are here in New Hope, so be it."

"But Goody Goodman?" Pastor Sanderson asked from the front row. He and his wife kept Constance, their adopted child, between them. "If she's a witch, then so could any of us."

"I'm glad you agree."

The voice pierced the air like a freshly whetted scythe through rye. The crowd parted, leaving a clear line in the straw leading up to the dark, thin man, the very subject of the meeting.

"Good evening."

"Evening, Reverend Michael," Mr. Hiddlesby barely uttered, the man's sudden presence pressing on his chest like a landslide of rocks. "If you need to speak with me about something, I'm in a meeting. I'll be free to talk to you in the morning."

"Oh, is this not an open forum?" Reverend Michael asked, his surprise sounding feigned. "My mistake. I couldn't help listening in; angry voices carry so well on the air. I don't suppose there is something I could do to help." He made a half-turn to the right, then to the other side as if looking for volunteers. "No? There must be something I can do." He opened his arms in welcome.

"Yes, you can leave," an unknown voice called.

"Ah, a revelation," the witch-hunter said with a nod. "I see, this meeting is about me. It is not the first time that God's will have been questioned." Turning away from Mr. Hiddlesby, he addressed the masses. "I understand that to some, my methods are severe, cruel even. But a little pain must be mete if the healing process is to begin. Slivers must be pulled out, bones reset, and debris cleansed from wounds."

Irked how Reverend Michael had taken control so smoothly, Mr. Hiddlesby retorted, "Yes, your methods concerns us, but also whether your company is necessary. I have received no proof that a witch resides in New Hope."

"Did anyone question the origins of the cat and mouse influx months ago? How do you explain those phenomena?"

"Swamp gas," a voice pipped.

"Earthquakes."

"Solar flares."

"Weather patterns."[44]

The witch-hunter snorted. "Preposterous. Witchcraft is the only answer."

This caused an uproar, but the tide was turning.

"There must be another answer."

"No, he's right. That wasn't natural."

"But a witch? In New Hope?"

"But who would do such a thing?"

Mr. Hiddlesby waved his hands, trying to calm the rising panic "If you are right about a witch being here, surely it isn't Goody Goodman. She's lived here for over a decade, and nothing like that has happened until now. It must be a mistake."

"What about Edith Partridge? She had her baby in jail," a woman called out.

"If Goody Goodman gave up Edith Partridge's

---

[44] The people who said these things didn't know why they said them; they just sounded like a good idea.

name, then it was out of coercion."[45]

"Or because she's a bit addled. You can't take what she says seriously."

The rivalry between the two women was legendary in New Hope. Edith Partridge was a notorious busy-body, poking her nose in everyone's dirty laundry to report back to her minister. Goody Goodman, in returned, was prone to spread rumors or play tricks on the large women, using her age to pretend senility.

Others nodded.

A priest jumped in. "Faithful Goodman is an upstanding member of my congregation. She hasn't missed a Sabbath meeting as far as I remember."

"The thing about witches," the witch-hunter began, "is that they are crafty, deceitful creatures. They could be anywhere, be anyone. They are patient, able to lie in wait for the right moment to attack Godly people when they are weak." His voice was low, soft. He sounded like a parent at bedtime, telling a cautionary tale.

"Witches can be anyone: our neighbor, an old woman, even someone as seemingly innocent as a child. They'll spread their evil in the cracks of our faith, weaseling in with small mischief, things we wouldn't think twice about, like chickens stopping to lay eggs and cows going dry. The witches will send bad dream, bad thoughts, bad air to you at night; target you when you can't defend yourself. They can come to you as specters, leaving their bodies behind. They attack the strong, the weak, the old, the young.

---

[45] For Reverend Michael, coercion wasn't exactly a bad thing.

Who knows how many of you are being afflicted right now by a witch. Your husband. Your wife. Your children. Your babies. And the most dangerous thing is that they want you to believe in one little lie: There are no witches in New Hope."[46]

Mr. Hiddlesby could see the effects of the reverend's speech ripple through the crowd like a rock being thrown in a pond. Heads knocked together, whispering, trading information. Suspicious eyes roamed the crowd. Fear flashed here and there.

The reverend had won over most of the people with his dark words. The only ones that weren't swayed by this rhetoric were the ministers of the churches, who brooded in silence. They didn't like a stranger coming into their town and sowing fear among their congregations.[47] They were still on Hiddlesby's side.

"Now, see here, Reverend. That's enough," the magistrate called, hoping to break the trance of the crowd. "You've gone far enough. You may see signs of a witch, but you can't accuse good women of such acts without solid proof."

Reverend Michael didn't react to any of this, merely glanced at the speakers, but for the most part, kept his attention singly on Mr. Hiddlesby. When the crowd died down, he asked the magistrate, "Sir, is your belief in these women stronger than your belief in God?"

The magistrate had never heard the phrase

---

[46] We've got some kind of trouble here in New Hope with a capital "W" that stands for witch.

[47] That was their job!

"loaded question," but he received an education of them that moment. "Er…there's nothing I believe in more than the Lord."

The crowd nodded. An obvious answer.

"I believe you. You strike me as a man who takes his job seriously, being a God-fearing man." The reverend smiled as if he'd made a joke. "I assure you, I am also a God-fearing man who takes my profession seriously. Let us not trespass where we don't belong."

Mr. Hiddlesby could read between the lines; he'd been politely told to mind his own business. If the reverend had been a different man, the magistrate may have gone toe to toe with him. If this had been an in-court proceeding, he'd have thrown the reverend into the jailhouse alongside Edith Partridge for contempt.

Which is what he was about to do, but then he took a look at the crowd. There was anger, as expected, but also worry and fear. There was a circle of empty space between the witch-hunter and everyone else. The barn had been crowded before, yet the people of New Hope refused to creep closer to Reverend Michael.

And someone had said that he was taking names. Which names did the witch-hunter have? Who would be next?

Mr. Hiddlesby straightened up. Standing on the wagon box, his head was higher than anyone else's, but he felt as if the witch-hunter was looking down on him. "The citizens have appointed me to uphold the law. I believe you have made your case about there being a witch in New Hope. From now on, as magistrate, I'll take over. If you will hand over all your findings, I will continue the search for any witches, if there are more. I'm sure a professional like you—"

"Have you studied the law?"

"Er…yes, I have." It was what made him more qualified than anyone else to be mayor and magistrate. Even the territory's legislated officials had thought so.

"So have I, that is, before I accepted a higher calling." Reverend Michael paced in the straw but kept his eyes on Mr. Hiddlesby. "Did you ever study God's law?"

"Ah…no. Just Sunday school."

"A pity. You see, witchcraft is unique as it borders both sets of laws. If you capture a murderer, does he have knowledge of other murderers? No. If you catch a thief, does he have knowledge of other thieves? Unlikely. There are few laws of the land that cross over to God's law, and none that require the finesse of finding other sinners, sinners that corrupt others like a festering wound. Wounds like those, the rotting flesh must be cut out."

Mr. Hiddlesby sensed that the crowd was hanging on the witch-hunter's every word, like a man clinging to a cliff before falling to his death.

Reverend Michael turned, addressing the town. "I know there are many among you who have spent their lives learning and living God's law. Of you men, are there any who have studied man's law as well? Anyone?"

No one spoke.

"No? Well, it seems that you are short of qualified professionals in this area. Witches are a crafty sort, and it takes one who is versed in both sets of laws to know how to deal with them."

Backed into a corner, Mr. Hiddlesby realized that he had underestimated the witch-hunter, thinking that the power of an official was enough to put the stranger in his place. But in a few minutes, Reverend Michael had just appointed himself as the only expert in witch-hunting and the final say-so in anything regarding the subject.

But the magistrate wasn't about to relinquish his position so easily.

"I am the judge of this township. I have been appointed by a higher legislature to govern the laws, and I am the only one to pronounce judgement on anyone, witches included," Mr. Hiddlesby said, pulling rank, satisfied that this would be the final word.

Reverend Michael waved a gracious hand, as if to resign. "Ah, I understand. As a judge of this land, you are held accountable to others. You report to a higher court, and you are worried what they would think if you ceded the law to a complete stranger. Yes, I can see why you are concerned."

Mr. Hiddlesby relaxed, feeling as if this was the end of it.

"YOU report to men, and it is their approval you seek. You should be more concerned with whom I report to; it is His approval you should seek. You said before that you put your faith in the Lord above all."

Mr. Hiddlesby could physically feel his power drain away from him to fill a larger pool that was Reverend Michael. It was then that he knew just why his cousin sounded so worried in the letter. That was an understatement. This man, this witch-hunter, was beyond reckoning. This was not a man to cross. Mr. Hiddlesby didn't want to cross this man or cross in front of him while walking down the street. He didn't even want to cross the territory the reverend lived in.

The sooner this man left New Hope, the better.

Looking among the crowd, he could see that nobody was willing to stand up to him. They were already regarding him as the top authority, the final word, of the town.

Sighing, the magistrate could do nothing but stay in his corner. "You have…clarified my misunderstandings. It is best that all witches be unveiled and brought to justice. I suppose there could be one or two more."

"Or more."

"More?"

"More. This reminds me; the jailhouse will need to be expanded. I'll need more cells."

He was taking names. How many more?

"Don't…Try not to…" The magistrate attempted to put his thoughts into words that couldn't be used against him, but it was impossible.

But the reverend was already walking away, needing no more permission than that.

*   *   *

It's not that Reverend Michael was surprised by the discontent in New Hope or the meeting that happened behind his back; no, that was to be expected. It was that it had been so easy to arrest away the magistrate's influence. Authority was a fragile thing if one didn't know how to wield it.

Now that that was out of the way, the real work could commence. The seeds were already planted; he could see the fear in the townsfolk. The witches knew he was coming. Even though he was a stranger, he was a quick learner of faces in this small town. Of the names that Edith Partridge gave him, one was Thou-Will-Be-Done Matson. It was ironic that the meeting took place in his barn.

Unlike Faithful and Edith, Thou-Will's witchiness wasn't obvious. The barn was neat and clean, and the animals seemed to be well cared for. Even his neighbors had been lacking in affliction. But the word was, since Thou-Will's farm was the closest to New Hope's center, his farm had been hit the hardest by the mice, and therefore, had the most cats. This was a sign.

However, considering the unrest of the town and how reliant everyone was on the farmers working in the fields, now was not the time to bring in Thou-Will.

In the meantime, there were plenty of other names on the list. He would be far from the devil's playground during his stay in New Hope. He walked slowly from the barn, pleased to see how the people trickled out as if reluctant to follow. His respect was rising.

"Reverend. Excuse me, reverend."

Surprised that anyone would attempt to talk to him after that performance, Reverend Michael turned around with dignity. "Yes?"

The plump man that approached him had the appearance of one who was used to having money. Even his handshake felt expensive. "Thomas Biddle. Proprietor of Biddle's General Store. I had to come introduce myself to you. Sir, that was quite a speech you gave in there, yes indeed. It ruffled some feathers, but that's just what this town needs."

The plump man, sweating in the afternoon heat, took off his hat and dabbed his balding head. What strands of hair he had left were a light brown. Or could it be red? Reverend Michael studied the color carefully before the hat was replaced. He didn't pass judgement just then and waited for Mr. Biddle to continue.

"When them cats came into town, I thought to myself, that just ain't natural. But, of course, nobody realized until your expertise saw it for what it was. Such a shame. New Hope is such a nice place. We certainly don't need witches ruining things."

Reverend Michael said nothing. He was still determining Biddle's character.

If Thomas Biddle was cowed by the witch-hunter's silence and intense stare, he hid it well. "As much as I respect Hiddlesby, he doesn't have the fire to do what must be done. Sometimes it takes a bigger man to take charge and make changes. You, sir, are that man. And I'd like to help out where I can."

The witch-hunter raised an eyebrow. The conversation became more fascinating. "I don't suppose you have witnessed any more black magic other than the cats. Perhaps sensed someone cursing you? Or seen someone suspicious walking around at night?"

The plump merchant chuckled as if the witch-hunter told a joke. "Nope, not a thing. Runnin' a store is my business. I wouldn't ask you to help me stock my shelves, now would I? No, of course not. Your business is witch-huntin', and I wouldn't know what to look for. I know nothin' about that. What I know is products, and I'd like to help your cause anyway I can. You mentioned extending the jailhouse. Well, let me donate wood and nails to get that started. And if there's anythin' else I can do, you just come on down to Biddle's General Store and ask for me. I'll get you set up."

Seeing now what kind of man Mr. Biddle was, Reverend Michael nodded, having determined that his hair must be brown, not the devilish fire-color that he had suspected. Of course, being wealthy didn't help the man's cause, but not everyone's failings had roots in witchcraft. "That is very generous of you, Mr. Biddle. Your tithe will vastly help the Lord's work. Depending on how long I stay in New Hope, I may call on your offer."

They shook again; Thomas Biddle's grip felt like a contract.

Heading back to the inn, Reverend Michael knew that the Lord worked in mysterious ways and sometimes gave His servants the easy path. If what he suspected was true, that a large coven of witches resided in New Hope, he would need more than his apprentice as an ally and he couldn't count on Phinchas Partridge with his wife right there in the jail. He needed associates. Thomas Biddle would be the first of many.

*   *   *

A man of his word, Thomas Biddle sent over the supplies the next day. Reverend Michael gave Phinchas Partridge the task of building more cells; the jailhouse guard argued about this assignment, considering that his job description consisted of putting people in jail and guarding them,[48] and nobody ever said anything about building things with hammer and nails, and perhaps there needs to be someone with a job where he could go complain about this, something with "Human" in the title, maybe "Resources." But the witch-hunter turned down any of those suggestions, his eyes draining in color with anger.

It turned out to be the best command Reverend Michael gave, especially with the man's wife in jail. Over the cries of the new-born Partridge and the nine other caged progeny, Edith kept a stream of orders at her husband for the extra rooms. Never had New Hope seen Phinchas move so quickly in his life.

With the menial tasks out of the way, Reverend Michael and his apprentice concentrated on the list of names. As most logical people do, he started at the top. Before week's end, he had Ida Vassal and Temperance Firman brought in for questioning due to the obvious signs that they were witches. Brooms,

---

[48] Most of the time, the jail was empty, so, for the most part, his job was optional.

cats, and one of them even had the nerve to have red hair.[49]

Both these women denied their association with black magic at first, as was expected, but after an hour or two with the lacquered box, they saw the error of their ways, dictating a novel of indecencies while under the influence of the Devil. They gave names, most similar to what Edith Partridge had admitted with a few extra. The two witches joined Edith and her children, which were now sharing two cells, more still being constructed.

Having been in New Hope for two weeks, Reverend Michael learned more of those on his most wanted list. While the others seemed small potatoes,[50] he was highly interested in Goody Stanford, who had the reputation of healing wounds and sicknesses with plants and herbs.[51] While the idea of using flora for healing isn't unholy or a new concept, he was sure she was a witch because she was actually good at her job. Plus, she had funny ideas about women finding employment and having a say in things. Witchcraft in its unadulterated form.

Unfortunately, since Goody Stanford's husband died ten years ago, she hadn't remained in New Hope, taking on the role of wanderer, searching the wilderness for her potion ingredients, and healing anyone who needed it. No doubt, she portrayed herself as the benevolent widow just to spread her

---

[49] Everyone knows that red-heads are soulless servants of the devil, even if not all are witches.
[50] You know, the witches who are only experimenting or only using the gateway spells.
[51] How dare she!

choking weeds of black magic wherever she went.

With no Goody Stanford to set his sights on, he continued down the list to Thou-Will-Be-Done Matson. He was cautious, considering that Thou-Will was an upstanding member[52] in the small community; he needed more than the usual irrefutable facts and evidence.[53]

After diving into the gossip pool, it came as no surprise to learned that Thou-Will had been married before; his first wife died early in their marriage. Not only that, but the present Goody Matson had been unable to conceive, and the couple remained childless in their five years of marriage. The lack of children was obviously indicative of witchcraft.[54] And the final nail in the coffin, it was rumored that Thou-Will had traveled to distant, foreign lands[55] as a boy. You had to be careful with those foreign lands; witchcraft was accepted as the norm, even encouraged, in other places.[56]

While it wasn't uncommon for a man to be a witch, it wasn't usual.[57] It was no secret that the female of the species dipped their feet more often in the pool of sin. In the witch-hunter's eyes, being female automatically moved them three steps closer to Satan. It had something to do with the moon and

---

[52] And a man besides.

[53] Finger-pointing, brooms, cats, the whole nine yards.

[54] Although some would argue the other way around.

[55] The kind of places where they believed in more than one god and ran around with less clothing than what was decent.

[56] It probably had to do with wearing less clothing.

[57] Or natural. Not that witches were natural to begin with, but a male witch was even less so.

cycles. One would think this proof that the system was faulty,[58] but why argue with biology.

This was Reverend Michael's first time interrogating a male witch. As expected, Thou-Will turned out to be a stubborn man, refusing to turn to the light and repent, even under the direction of the reverend's lacquered box. After hours of interrogation, Reverend Michael conceded defeat. Not every soul was meant to be saved.

At this point in the investigation, Reverend Michael wanted to send the witch—or warlock in this case—to the gallows, but with the whole town watching him closer than a weasel after a chicken, he thought that this was the right time to make a public example, to show that there were indeed witches among them.

The next day, he announced to the town that a ducking would be administered to Thou-Will to determine the man's guilt.[59] Word spread like germs in a classroom, and everyone made sure to be there with a macabre sense of curiosity.

The point of the ducking would be to determine through scientific means if Thou-Will was a witch by throwing him in the river. If he floated, that would prove he was a witch, and then he'd be hanged. If he

---

[58] One woman in Hartford disputed Reverend Michael for his beliefs that the fairer sex should be referred as the errant sex, saying he was sexist and unrighteous. The reverend briskly won that argument by pointing his infamous finger and pronouncing her a witch. She was immediately carted away for the public to throw rotten fruits and vegetables that they kept handy for such occasions.

[59] Or innocence. Whatever.

sank and drowned, his innocence would be proven and his soul would fly straight to heaven.[60]

The day of Thou-Will's trial was one that nobody would forget, least of all Reverend Michael.

*   *   *

Constance wasn't sure why her aunt and uncle dragged her to the river. The river scared her. Almost all water scared her. Not water that you drank from a cup. As long as it came from a cup, it was trustworthy. A bath was fine. In fact, as long as water was in some sort of container, you knew where it stood. It wasn't going to splash or surprise you.

But rivers, that was wild water. It didn't do anything predictable. You never knew how deep it was, how fast it was moving, how cold it was just by looking at it. It could do anything.

There was a large crowd around the river. Constance hated crowds as well. Crowds were a lot like rivers; even if they were made of civil, good people, they could still turn feral.

Even though her aunt and uncle told her that Lucifer wouldn't want to go, the cat followed anyway. He was a cat, and nobody could tell him where he didn't want to go. On the off chance that he could understand human talk, he probably would follow just to prove this point. Even with the proximity of the river and hundreds of tail-stomping boots, Lucifer stayed loyally close to the young woman.

---

[60] A win-win situation.

Keeping to the outskirts, Constance played with her cornhusk dolls in the dust while other children younger and older than her watched with wide eyes as the witch-hunter paraded Thou-Will Matson around.

Constance liked Thou-Will. Most adults felt uncomfortable around her, but not Thou-Will. He always had a kind word for her and small gifts that she cherished, like an abandoned bird's nest or a piece of honeycomb. She had even looked him in the eye a time or two.

When she caught a glimpse of Thou-Will in the state he was in, tied hand and foot with rope, bags under his eyes, bleeding from the sharp instruments of torture and bruised from the needle that refused to draw blood, she became agitated. Still clutching her crude playthings, she rocked back and forth, moaning softly. Lucifer, like a soldier, took his place in her lap, purring like a thunderstorm and glaring at anyone who dared comment.

She tried to ignore the noise of the crowd, the sound of the witch-hunter's angry voice, and the fear radiating off of the townsfolk.

Then Thou-Will was thrown into the river, heaved like a fishing net, and disappeared under the water.

Constance screamed.

*   *   *

Thou-Will did not fear the witch-hunter. He hated the scarecrow of a man and how he twisted the truth to suit his purposes. His first wife had died of typhoid, which he blamed himself for. When he married Catharine and she couldn't conceive, he blamed himself for that, too. Yes, he had also traveled to foreign lands. His uncle was a ship merchant and had taken him on many long voyages. He had been all over Europe, several parts of Africa, and dozens of small islands. He had seen the dark-skinned natives perform their religious dances, slaughter animals to unknown gods, and even perform spells.

But he was not a witch. He had been faithful his whole life, even after being driven from England by ignorance, starting anew in a strange world, and having one wife torn away from him. He had known, just as his name reminded him, that the Lord's will would be done.

He just was unsure what the Lord's will was.

Thou-Will was not a big man. He was tall, but as thin as a wolf in winter, muscles hardened from daily labor in the fields. He had always been this way since a boy. He had learned to swim with pearl divers on exotic islands, and since he had no fat on his bones, he sank like a rock weighted down by an anchor.

He knew he would sink. The river was over fifteen feet deep. Even in his weakened condition, it wouldn't be hard for him to keep afloat by treading water as he had been taught.

But he didn't intend to swim. If he did, not only would he be hung for being a witch, but the scrutinizing eyes of the witch-hunter would turn to Catharine. He wanted to sink for his wife, for the whole town to know that there are no witches.

He was sure that was the Lord's will.

When his body was thrown in and he sank, he relaxed, feeling the peace of several feet of water separating him from the tumultuous world. He tried to keep track of how long he held his breath, but his burning lungs and cloudy mind distracted him. He had been down for at least two minutes, maybe more, he was sure. When he couldn't hold his air anymore, he slowly released it, feeling the bubbles retreat to the surface.

His chest ached to refill, and he struggled against his body's need. He knew that once he inhaled, that would be the end. It wouldn't take him long to die.

Then a voice spoke to him, just as clear as if someone whispered in his ear, calling his name.

*   *   *

The witch-hunter loved a good ducking. In Boston, it sometimes turned into a fair, some placing bets on whether the person would float or sink. Not that Reverend Michael condoned gambling or revelry of any kind, but it made him feel better if the crowd was cheery. He just hoped that the town's somber attitude wouldn't ruin it for him when the witch's head popped to the surface like a cork, ensuring his triumph.

He enjoyed himself when he watched his apprentice heave Thou-Will into the river, but the moment was ruined when that strange girl with the ungodly beast screamed her head off. He glared in her direction, wondering what a child her age was doing crying like a baby. Not even her guardians could calm her, which went to show that they had no discipline at all.

"Take her away," he commanded, flinging his arm toward the town.

That was what was wrong with New Hope. No discipline. When restraint went out the window, you might as well open your door to Satan and his hell brides and invite them to tea.

By the time Thou-Will had been under for two minutes, the crowd had become restless, doubting the trial. They doubted him.

"He must be dead," someone whispered nearby.

Reverend Michael felt their judgmental eyes on him, blaming him. He didn't turn to look at the nay-sayers; his eyes were cemented to the river, willing for something to happen.

After three minutes, several women were crying. Many crossed themselves, saying the prayers of the deceased.

Catharine Matson sobbed as women do without regard for the people around them.[61] "Please," she cried, turning to Reverend Michael. "Is this not enough for you? He did not float to the top. Proclaim his innocence, I beg you. He is no witch. He may still live."

"If he still lives, then it is because of witchcraft," Reverend Michael said darkly.

Another woman pulled Goody Matson away, glaring at the witch-hunter. "Must you be so indifferent? The woman is now a widow. At least allow someone to retrieve the body for burial."

Every second that Thou-Will didn't float only confirmed this and brought more and more of the

---

[61] They could be so insensitive.

town against the witch-hunter. Appeasement was in order.

"Brothers and sisters, it is my deepest regret that we have lost another soldier of God's army to the forces of darkness," Reverend Michael began, ad-libbing a eulogy. He wasn't this kind of reverend, but it wasn't beyond his expertise. "Thou-Will was, indeed, innocent of this crime against nature and against God. As we pray for his soul, which we know is on his way to the Lord's embrace, we must allow Thou-Will's death to be a cautionary tale to us all. If it weren't for the witches that reside in New Hope, he would be with us still."

Then he launched into reciting the Lord's Prayer, seeing the crowd bow their heads in mournful silence. Before he finished, a woman screamed, pointing behind him to the water. Thinking that it was only Thou-Will's body finally rising, he only turned when he heard the desperate sounds of gasping.

A few more women screamed, some fainted.

"My husband," Catharine Matson shouted, racing to the bank to pull her nearly-dead spouse out of the water. She wasn't strong enough, so two men helped her.

As pale as the drowned, Thou-Will tried to speak, his words, at first, little more than wheezes. When he found his voice, he rasped, "Under the…water…someone…called my name…Who called my name?"

Catharine, weeping, said through her sobs, "Nobody spoke your name. All was silent except for the reverend."

"But I heard someone say…Thou-Will-Be-Done," the gasping man said.

"And it was," a voice from the crowd said.

There were shouts of joy, cheering, even cries that a miracle had happened that day.

Reverend Michael didn't believe it. Thou-Will had been in the river for five minutes, maybe six. No mortal man could have survived that long. At least, not without the dark arts.

And even with this scathing evidence, he could do nothing.

Grabbing his apprentice, Reverend Michael marched to New Hope, the fires of indignation burning in his chest. He had been tricked![62] Thou-Will was a stronger witch than he thought for the Devil to use such power to save his servant.

"I acted too brash," he told his apprentice.

The boy could barely keep up with his long-legged master. "To think, doing that to someone who wasn't a witch," the apprentice said.

"Of course he's a witch. I was tricked into thinking he was already dead," the witch-hunter shouted. "I was a fool. It is unforgiveable that I've allowed a witch to walk free."

"But…can't we just…you know…tell everyone

---

[62] He never forgot the incident and from that point, refused to use ducking on any witch. Reverend Michael even preached against it to his peers, proclaiming it not to be "Devil-proof" and a chance for witches to "get away with it." His words went unheeded until a witch-hunter down in the Carolinas threw a largely obese woman into a river and thought he had won as she floated quite easily. He was celebrating so much, he neglected to fish her out, so she floated away out of his reach.

it was a mistake?" the apprentice asked with a shrug.

"After pronouncing his innocence? It would ruin my reputation. I will not sully God's work with my mistake," Reverend Michael pronounced. "You know, my parents named me after the archangel, Michael. That is why I chose to hunt witches. Most men of the cloth, they prefer the work of peace. It takes more than a desire to serve to take up a flaming sword and fight God's enemies."

This was the reason he went by this name instead of Reverend Boggust. Michael was a name that people respected, that brought up religious, glorifying images from scripture passages. It was a name a witch-hunter could use with confidence.[63]

"Oh," the apprentice said noncommittally.

The witch-hunter often wondered about his apprentice. The boy did as was told and seemed keen on the work, but perhaps he didn't have the instincts. There was a reason the boy was his seventh apprentice.

"We won't let this mishap remain a disadvantage," Reverend Michael said in a conspiratorial tone. "He believes that I no longer suspect him, and we shall keep it that way."

"Why?"

"To spy on him."

The apprentice looked wary. "How?"

"From now on, I'll have you run many errands,

---

[63] Boggust, on the other hand, only brought up images of ghoulish, dark things that crept around under beds and in closets, which for most who met Reverend Michael, may have said fit him better than Michael.

lots and lots of them, all around the vicinity of Thou-Will's home. You shall take note of everyone with whom he and his wife make contact. There are more witches in this town, you can be sure of that."

*   *   *

The next day, as per instructed, the apprentice slowly walked by Thou-Will's farmhouse, carrying a package that had nothing in it. He had constructed several props of varying shapes and sizes to lug around while in the area. It was going to be tedious pacing between the jailhouse and Thou-Will's place on invisible errands, but he was willing to go through these lengths. Not only was he feeling confident and proud that Reverend Michael finally entrusted him with such an important task, but he was glad to be away from the cells and the prisoners. The convicted witches were a dull and depressing lot.

However, on his fifth "errand", he had yet to see any suspicious activity. Disappointed that he hadn't caught a glimpse of one spell or demon—or at the very least, another person—he was determined not to return to his master without something to report. Abandoning his empty package, he glanced around for any prying eyes—besides his own—before slipping behind a tree.

But he had been observed from above. A cold sweat flowed down his back and neck when he heard a rumbling, as if thunder was rolling closer, but there wasn't a cloud in the sky. Searching for the origins of the sound, he spotted it in the branches of the tree. A single eye peered down at him, belonging to the same scruffy, three-legged, half-tailed kitten—Tripod—he saved from drowning.[64]

"Go away," he hissed at Tripod. Then remembering what his master would think of one who talked to cats, he turned away from the feline.

Ignoring a cat is the best way to catch its attention.

The apprentice screamed as a weight fell on his head, causing him to flail his arms before collapsing from the attack.

Back on the ground, Tripod scampered away with a jerky kind of limp-run, which was faster than one would give the poor creature credit.

"Odin, there you are, you bad kitty. Was it you that made that awful noise?" A lilting voice carried on the air, the scolding sounding more sweet than angry. "I snuck some cream for you."

Lifting his head, the apprentice focused on the direction of the voice. When he saw the face that went with it, he felt as if something else dropped on his head, his heart spinning, dizzy.

Her hair was the color of honey and her smile looked just as sweet; together, they should have attracted a swarm of bees big enough to carry her off. She wasn't the prettiest girl he had ever seen; Boston had enough of those. But something about the slope of her nose, how she carried her head like a deer, graceful and calm, and how humble she looked in the rural surroundings, she was beautiful. Standing in the yard of Thou-Will's closest neighbor, she put down the dish she carried and scratched the gray kitten's—

---

[64] From his own hands, but saving is saving.

now named Odin—as it gobbled the treat.

The shock of seeing the young woman had distracted him from his pain, but it rushed back to him like high tide. A groan crept up his throat, but he wasn't sure if he should make a sound on account he was a spy, so it came out as, "Uuuuuugghh?"

It was enough to catch the attention of the girl, who came rushing. "Sir, sir, are you hurt?"

Feeling like the worst spy in the world, the apprentice rigidly stood up, brushing his black clothing—now marred with dirt and leaves—and straightening his hair. "I'm fine, miss. Just…had a scare. That cat surprised me."

"Oh, so that's what I heard." The girl giggled. "I do apologize. Odin is such a scamp. I think he intentionally scares people out of amusement. He can usually get a good scream out of mother on her way to the outhouse."

The apprentice laughed, glad he wasn't the only one that a three-legged, half-tailed, one-eyed kitten gotten the best of.

"Oh, my. You're that boy who's always with the witch-hunter," the girl noticed, hand going to her breast.

"I'm his apprentice," he corrected, frowning at being called a boy. Some considered eighteen to be a man.

"Oh, so that means one day, you'll be a witch-hunter as well?"

The way she asked, it seemed almost teasing, but not in a mean way. More in a way as if she were running her fingers through his hair to give him chills. He had a sudden desire for her to do just that.

"Yes, I suppose so. I just started in May, but I expect that I'll be one in no time," he bragged. Hoping to impress her, he added, "I started out in Boston. We hunted loads of witches there."

Her eyes widened, excited and fearful at the same time. "Did you see any of them ride their broom? Or cast any spells?"

He wanted to say yes just to please her, but he didn't want to lie. "One gave me the evil eye once," he compromised. It wasn't a fib. Through all the glares and angry looks, one was bound to be evil. "I wasn't scared. Reverend Michael says as long as I'm pure, I have nothing to fear."

"I would have thought to sprinkle some holy water on you," the girl offered.

The apprentice scowled. "That's something only Catholics do."

The girl lowered her head and drew back due to his tone. It was obvious what religion she belonged to.

"Sorry," the apprentice muttered. He knew there was some dislike between the Puritans and the Catholics, this fissure more obvious since he had taken with Reverend Michael. He had nothing against Catholics, but his master's views had rubbed off on him. "I'm sure it would have helped."

His words brought a smile back on her lips, and he knew he never wanted it to leave.

"I could bring you a bottle of holy water if you want. It will protect you."

He nodded readily, even if he had no idea what made water holy or how to use it.

"Come back tomorrow, and I'll have it."

So he did. And he came back the next day for some salt. And the next day for a picture of Jesus on the cross that she drew just for him. And the next day, even though she had nothing to give him, he came.

Her name was Sarah O'Conner, and he was certain she was a witch. She had done something to him, something that made him soft and squishy inside, made his bones unstable, his heart achy, and his thoughts go faster than…well…thought. She had put a spell on him, somehow, that kept bringing him back to her. Perhaps it was her smile. Or maybe it was the cat that attached the spell to him since the creature never left her side.

He didn't care. Except a part of him worried that his master would find out that his "spying" was really going to see Sarah. Oh, he did keep watch over Thou-Will's home, but mostly he watched her. He was petrified that Reverend Michael would know of Sarah's influence and see her for what she was.

And he had to make sure that the witch-hunter would never find out.

*   *   *

After the Thou-Will fiasco, Reverend Michael redoubled his fight against evil. With his apprentice off on his secret mission,[65] he took on Thomas Biddle as an assistant. The businessman took to the work like a male lion after driving off an old rival. He could walk the walk, talk the talk, accuse the accused. It

---

[65] Which took up so much time, Reverend Michael hardly ever saw him.

was an added bonus that he knew the citizens. He had an eye for spotting the signs. Questionable mole? Witch. Stuttering over the Lord's Prayer? Witch. Rhyming over a bubbling cauldron? Witch. It was as if Biddle was born for this.

They did not lack people to bring in. The more witches they interrogated, the more names they added. Phinchas Partridge built more cells and even started on a courtroom attached to the jailhouse. The courtroom wasn't fancy, a few rows of benches, a box for the accused to stand in, and a platform where Reverend Michael could pace as he played the role of prosecutor, judge, and jury. He would also take on the role of executioner if given the chance, but not since Thou-Will's ducking had anyone fought against the charges of witchcraft longer than a day.

With the outdoor courtroom in use, the town took advantage of this unusual entertainment, filling the crude benches every day. Most watched, but others took the opportunity to fill the parts of the witnesses and victims, with a little bit of coaching. Most didn't know they were being harassed by witches until Reverend Michael educated them. Who knew that accidents, unknown ailments, bad luck, strange dreams, and sinful thoughts were all because of a witch? It was so nice for them to comprehend where the blame was supposed to go.

It was in the pinnacle of this witch season where Reverend Michael tried a new witch every day that Goody Stanford, the herbalist, returned to New Hope.

Reverend Michael, through Thomas Biddle, had learned enough to convict her on sight. Leah Stanford had only been married to her husband for a week before he succumbed to consumption. Instead of remarrying, she earned her living by selling medicinal plants throughout the colonies. She claimed New Hope as her home, refusing to sell her nuptial house where she stayed during the winter months. On top of that, she educated women, taught them to read, to stand up for themselves, and to defend themselves if necessary. She spoke of bizarre things like women's rights, even claiming that a woman could do anything a man could if she set her mind to it.

Dangerous thinking, that was. A witch in anyone's book.[66]

The second Goody Stanford put a toe in New Hope's boundaries, Reverend Michael arrested her. Even though several women and three men were in line for trial, he bumped up her to the front.[67]

*   *   *

Goody Stanford didn't mind being put in jail. She was just glad to be among people again, so the screaming Partridge clan and the other witches didn't bother her. She was even lucky enough to have several cures. Times had been hard for her lately. Mass hysteria kept people wary of her wares, even those who had known her for years. But the people in the New Hope jail had no worries; they were already

---

[66] Most would look at this story and think, *This woman obviously isn't a witch. That would be too cliché. And there are no such things as witches.* But anyone making this assumption would be wrong. Goody Stanford was a real witch; maybe the only true witch Reverend Michael ever put on trial.

[67] I'm sure the others didn't mind her getting priority treatment.

punished for being witches and benefitted from Goody Stanford's expertise. Before she was marched into the courtroom the next day, she had treated the Partridge baby's cough with a poultice, gave Benevoline Cribb a powder for her rheumatism, and cured Mr. Thompson's toe warts.[68]

Once placed in the accused box, a U formed of handrails on a raised platform, Goody Stanford watched calmly as the thin man faced her, his legs already adopting the pace for prosecuting, his finger poised to condemn.

Before he could say anything, she declared, "Yes, I am a witch."

"I-I'll lead this courtroom," Reverend Michael stuttered, frowning. He glanced at his audience. "Are you a witch, Mrs. Stanford?"

Goody Stanford paused as if to say, "Are you done?" before calmly replying, "Please, call me, Goody Stanford. And, yes, I am a witch."

"Since you have already confessed, we will do without the witnesses today and go right onto sentencing."

Many people on the benches groaned in disappointed, no more than those at the front who were going to be the witnesses for the day.

"What witnesses?" Goody Stanford asked, looking at the audience with disapproval.

"Your victims, of course," Reverend Michael said. "If you refused to acknowledge your transgression, all evidence needs to be presented to make my case against you."

---

[68] Which were, ironically, the thing that proved he was a witch.

"And what do these so-called witnesses say I did to them?"

A girl stood up. "She keeps pinching me." She yelped, clasping her backside. "Stop it. Ouch!"

The man and woman next to her pointed. He said, "She puts spells on our cows, makin' 'em dry up."

The woman nodded, her face as turned up as a pug's. "An' ay saws her kissin' the devil's be-hind."

This caused some tittering in the gallery.

An elderly man at the end of the bench declared, "She put unclean thoughts about her in my mind. She wants me and is using the Devil to get to me." He leered at her, waggling his eyebrows suggestively.

Goody Stanford didn't react, not even surprised by the allegations. Instead, she spoke as sternly as a school marm. "Euphadora, watching you grow up spoiled as you were, I'm not surprised that you have taken to slandering good folk in this parody of justice. If someone is indeed pinching your buttocks with their mind, you very well deserve it."

The girl sat down in shame.

The witch turned to the couple, looking even more severe. "Mr. and Mrs. Potts, I'm not surprised that you have run out produce. I have been telling you for years that your livestock is growing too old and that you give them substandard feed. If you don't treat your animals better, do not be surprised if they die."

The two gasped. "You hear that. She cursed our farm. She's a witch," the woman called out.

"Oh, stop it. Everyone in the town knows it. I'm just the only one who'll say anything about it,"

Goody Stanford snapped. Then she turned on the old man. "As for you Ezekia Kroggen, if I wanted to make a man desire me, it wouldn't be you, you daft fool. Sit down before you hurt yourself."

The old man chuckled, but did as was told.

Like a whip, her head snapped back to the witch-hunter. "I have confessed, but I won't let false witnesses be the ones to condemn me."

A voice from the crowd said, "'Thou shalt not bear false witness against thy neighbor.'"

"Nicely put, Constance. Thank you," Goody Stanford commented to the girl she couldn't see, for nobody else could have said it. "I'll be the witness of my own deeds, if you will, since I'm the only one who witnessed it."

The witch-hunter looked amused as if she were leading herself to the noose. "By all means."

"I cast a cat-summoning spell."

"Ah-ha! A cat—" Reverend Michael looked triumphant, then confused as if unsure why he exclaimed. "A cat-summoning spell?"

The crowd murmured amongst themselves. Goody Stanford hated to brag, but the town had the right to know what she had done.

"How do you think all those cats got here?"

"I'll be asking the questions," Reverend Michael insisted. "You have committed an egregious sin, you black-hearted, shriveled hag."

"Oh, calm down. No need to be uncivil," the witch sniffed. She wasn't exactly a young doe, but she wasn't some crone. "It was no sin. I used white magic."

"The Devil has lied to you. There's no such thing as white magic. Magic of all colors is the product of Satan."[69]

"How nice that Satan is no magical bigot," Goody Stanford joked, earning laughs from the gallery. "If anything was a product of the Devil, it was those mice."

The witch-hunter paced slower, considering. "Where did you get your cat-summoning spell? Did you sign your name in the Devil's ledger? Or did someone in New Hope give it to you?"

"No, a woman in Pennsylvania gave it to me. She was an Indian or at least part of one. I traded a slab of butter for it."

"And where does this woman live?"

Goody Stanford thought he looked like a cat waiting for a mouse. "I won't tell you. Now hush while I finish my story. It isn't polite to interrupt."

The witch-hunter snapped to attention as if she had slapped his hand for grabbing a cookie.

"I cast the spell to take care of the mice. I may not be the most faithful of Christians, but I don't think the Lord would condemn me for undoing that darkness."

"You cannot hide behind your twisted justification anymore, just as you cannot hide your misdeeds and the murder you covered up."

"What murder?" Goody Stanford demanded.

"The murder of your husband," Reverend Michael answered, assured. "One week is an awfully

---

[69] If you don't believe him, look into what a terror purple magic is.

short time for one to be married."

"Don't you dare…"

"Convenient, though, for a witch who wishes to be alone with nobody bothering her about marriage, no husband to walk in on her secret deeds. I have heard that many potions need ingredients from a dead man's body and grave."

"I did not murder my husband. His death…nearly destroyed me."

"Then why insist everyone call you Goody Stanford? Most drop the title of Goodwife once widowed. Why not be called Widow Stanford? Don't want another husband?"

"There's nothing wrong with not wanting to remarry," Goody Stanford defended. "Not that it's any of your business, but I kept the title of Goodwife because I remain to this day a faithful wife. In the eyes of the Lord, I am still married to my Willard, God rest his soul. This town remembers him, I hope fondly. If they do, they'll remember his kindness and charity, how he helped those in need. I keep his memories alive by doing the same thing. I dedicated my life to serving the less fortunate, even if that puts me in a bad light with others and condemn me to this, so be it."

She could see many in the town bow their heads, perhaps saying a prayer for her husband's soul or for a lost loved one.

The witch-hunter appeared to not have heard but plowed on with the farce of a trial. "It is to your credit that you have confessed to being a witch. It proves you haven't fallen too far from the Lord. I am willing to help you." He reached for his lacquered box as a man would reach for his Bible.

She had heard of this box filled with instruments of torture. The lacquered box had more of a reputation than the witch-hunter.

The audience looked more lively, excited by the turn of events.

"But for you to repent, you must give up the names of other witches."

"Now this kind of nonsense is why I came back to New Hope. Other witches, indeed. There is only one other, a bad one at that. There's a black witch in New Hope, and it was they that summoned the mice."

This caused an explosion of excitement as if the courtroom was an anthill that a child just kicked. It took several motions of Reverend Michael's hands to quiet them.

"You have a name? Only one? It would help your repentance process to give more."

"Are you listening? There's only one. There's only ever been one. These folks you've been terrorizing and locking up, they're innocent. If you weren't such a fool, you'd see it."

Reverend Michael's hands turned white from tightening his grip on the lacquered box. "You dare insult me? I'm Reverend Michael Be-Steadfast Fear-God Kill-Sin Boggust. I won't be talked to in such a manner."

"Careful, Reverend," Goody Stanford whispered so only he could hear. "Witchcraft may be punishable by death, but Pride is deadly."

Face turning puce, he ordered through clenched teeth, "Give me the name."

"I don't know it. I only know of the black witch because I found a talisman in the woods that brought the mice here. It was an ugly thing of twisted bones, hair, and beads covered in blood. I burned it as soon as I found it, which ended the spell. But it was too late; the plague of mice was already here. Which is why I used the cat-summoning spell."

After that, Goody Stanford could see a few faces change to that of gratitude, sorrow or pity. There were some that believed that her intentions were benevolent. Among these was her sister, Rachael Fontaine. She had ignored her sister all this time to protect Rachael. There was a small chance that nobody would inform the reverend of their family connection since they had different surnames, but it was unlikely. The best she could do was pretend they were estranged.

"How convenient," Reverend Michael sneered. "The prince of lies has taught you well."

"You aren't much of a witch-hunter, and you certainly are no truth-seeker with how many lies you've believed," Goody Stanford rounded. "Your witches are no more than an excuse for your power-mongering, trying to make a name for yourself by preying on the weakest of society, starting with the elderly, the poor, and those with no family, as I saw in the jailhouse. And don't think I didn't see you, Thomas Biddle, shadowing the reverend like a hungry wolf. Was putting Mr. Thompson in jail your idea? Isn't he your biggest competition? How convenient."

Those words, an echo of the witch-hunter's, brought a hush to the people.

"Don't listen to this serpent," Reverend Michael shouted, waving his arm. "She is sowing deception to divide us. But we must remain faithful." He turned his back on the woman to open his lacquered box, his body instantly calmed. "I believe that you came to repent, Goody Stanford, but it appears that Old Scratch is preventing you. But I can help you with your penance."

Goody Stanford pulled the hood of her large travel cloak over her head and leaned forward. "If anyone needs penance, it is you."

When the witch-hunter whirled around, he faced the accused box and a pile of clothing without a body in sight. Wide-eyed, he turned in tight circles as if she had run away or hid right behind him.

The audience was as aghast. One minute, they were watching the scene with abated breath, and the next, Goody Stanford's clothing collapsed as if she had disintegrated.

She had vanished.

*　　　　　*　　　　　*

Rachael Fontaine returned home from her sister's trial with shock and tears. Her husband had taken the children out into the fields to help with the late crops, and she was glad she could be alone. However, the house was not how she left it.

On the table were a handful of papers with the familiar scrawling of her sister's hand. Snatching them up, she read:

Dear Rachael,

By now you will know what I have done and what I am. Please do not fear for me. I have made peace for my decision, and I hope that you will as well. I don't know if God has forgiven me for casting the spell; I do not intend on using another, but if I had to do it all over again, I would do the same. I did it for you and Paul and your children. Please forgive me and pray for my soul, because while I am done with the spell, it is not done with me.

Not long after I cast the cat-summoning spell, I noticed changes to my body. Since then, I can see better in the dark, and I can hear farther than I had before. I found this peculiar, but not in the least alarming. It wasn't until I was climbing a tree to pick some apples that I grabbed a dead branch. Anyone would have fallen like a ragdoll and broken an arm or a leg or worse. However, I was able to twist in midair and land on my hands and feet.

The letter continued to relate the changes Leah had observed. She would sleep curled up in a ball. She became afraid of water. A desire to eat raw fish and chase mice haunted her daily thoughts. There were paragraphs that showed the battle she went through, her humanity fighting against these changes. The final stage of this metamorphosis was that cats began following her, traveling with her from town to town. Not only did they understand and obey her commands,[70] but she understood them in turn.

---

[70] At least when it wasn't too inconvenient. You know cats.

The final page read:

Everywhere I go, the cats follow. Their conversations are vain and insulting of everything and everyone, including their fellow cats. You wouldn't enjoy their conversations, but I have found them tolerable, even amiable in my wanderings.

Do not worry about me. I have chosen this path. I gave my life to God long ago, and I will continue to wander until he calls me home, if he allows me in. Perhaps it is better this way. You once compared my personality to that of a cat, and it will not be a bad end to live as one.

This is my last good-bye, my sister. Whatever happens today, I will not contact you again. I hope that evil does not fall on you because of me.

Give the little ones kisses from me.

Love,
Leah

After reading, Rachael placed her hands over her mouth, breathing heavily. It hurt to think of her sister, how she suffered all these months, worried about her immortal soul when she was only trying to help the town. After witnessing what happened in the courtroom, she wondered if Leah's sudden disappearance had to do with the changes. Had she…turned into a cat?

Nobody had been looking at the floor. A cat could easily have slipped away, unnoticed.

No sooner had she come to this conclusion that there was a knock at the door. Through the window, she glimpsed the familiar black clothing and Puritan hat. After a slight hesitation, she threw the letter into the stove with the hot coals, the paper bringing a flame to life.

Then she opened the door.

"Yes."

"Goody Fontaine?"

"Yes, that is me."

"Are you the sister of Leah Stanford?"

A bubble of fear rose in her breast. Remembering her sister's own bravery in facing the witch-hunter, she held her head high. "Yes."

"You must come with us for questioning under suspicion of witchcraft."

*   *   *

The next day, New Hope awoke to silence. After months of an overpopulation of felines that had caterwauled in the alleys, mewled at doorways for milk and scraps, and scratched at every tree, porch and pant leg, all were gone save for a few beloved pets, including the twenty-odd that refused to leave Faithful Goodman.[71]

Even with this eerie silence, the townsfolk took it as a good sign. After all, the cats had brought the witch-hunter to town, perhaps the exodus of felines would send him away.

---

[71] Some might even say the twenty-odd that Faithful Goodman refused to let go.

But it was quite the opposite. Reverend Michael saw this as a message from God: evil was fleeing. He was winning. It was time to turn it up a notch.

"Apprentice, get in here." After months of having the boy shout, "How high?" whenever he thought about the word "jump," it was like a concert missing its string section to not have the apprentice at his side immediately.

Of course, the apprentice was still watching Thou-Will's house. It pleased the reverend that the boy was committed to this assignment like a hound on a trail. He had misgivings about the apprentice at first, but this showed that he had the fervor for the work. However, at this moment, Reverend Michael wished that the boy didn't have so much fervor.

It wasn't until that afternoon that the apprentice returned.

"Apprentice, come here."

The boy rushed to him, just as eager to please as always. Maybe even more eager than before.

"Do you have anything to report?"

"Nothing new. Just that one girl and her cat again. She plays there all the time."

Reverend Michael recalled the face, or at least the fragment of a face that peered out through a curtain of unkempt hair. It was the same girl who owned that deranged cat, who screamed during Thou-Will's trial, who quoted scripture in the courtroom. However, the name of the girl escaped him.

"Unfortunately, I will need you for something else," Reverend Michael told the boy, scribbling down the list. "With Thomas Biddle leading the neighborhood witch-watch group looking for Goody

Stanford, I'll need you to bring these newly accused witches in for questioning." He handed over the list.

Reading the paper, the apprentice blanched. "Y-yes sir. I'll get on it first thing in the morning."

"Good lad."

*   *   *

New Hope used to be a haven for Constance with plenty of places filled with peace and quiet where she could play with Lucifer and her dolls, but, like the jailhouse, most of her favorite spots had become unfriendly, loud, and filled with fear. Ever since she saw Thou-Will thrown into the river, she used his property as a go-to; she worried that the river might get him again. Not only was Thou-Will and Catharine Matson kind to her and Lucifer, but their neighbors, specifically Sarah O'Conner and the kitten Odin, welcomed her anytime.

Constance usually determined a person's character by how much they liked cats, especially Lucifer. If a person didn't have enough kindness for the bedraggled feline, they weren't worth knowing.

It didn't take meeting the witch-hunter for Constance to know she didn't like him. She had the feeling that Lucifer would hate him, and she tried to stay as far away from him as possible. By association, she disliked the apprentice at first.

Constance had never changed her mind about anyone until Catharine told her she liked the witch-hunter apprentice. She could tell that the apprentice made Sarah happy. Odin liked him. Lucifer tolerated him. That was enough for Constance. She liked how the apprentice helped Sarah with her chores, how they laughed together, and how they both talked sweetly to Odin, Lucifer, and Constance.

Because of their laughter and kindness, Constance frequented Thou-Will's property more and more often, which was why she was there when the apprentice came twice in one day, his voice filled with urgency.

"Sarah. Sarah."

Sarah's mother, Mrs. O'Conner, greeted him, her lips pursed. Constance knew that meant she was displeased, but she didn't understand why. She was used to not understanding. Anger was just as foreign to her as witches.

"I need to see Sarah."

"I think you've used up enough of Sarah's time, young man," Mrs. O'Conner scolded.

It was all for naught since Sarah came running, her face dusted with flour. "I'll just be a minute, mama."

The woman's face looked like a squashed roll when she frowned.

Sarah and the apprentice moved away from the house to the tree that Odin liked to climb. Constance shuffled about, letting them know she was there. Odin followed and gave Lucifer a sniff, the latter only turned his back on the kitten, his way of saying he didn't want to play.

"We can talk here," Sarah stated.

"What about her?"

"She's no bother. Constance won't tell anyone what we'll say, will you, sweetie?" Sarah stroked Constance's brown hair.

She leaned away, but still smiled as she studied the ground. "'Whoso keepeth his mouth and his tongue keepeth his soul from troubles,'" Constance recited. Contrary to those who associated her with a parrot, she knew exactly what she meant when she quoted scripture.

"I think that's from Proverbs," Sarah explained. "It means she won't tell anyone."

The apprentice grabbed Sarah's shoulders, turning her to him. "Sarah, you're in danger. Reverend Michael has your name."

Sarah choked on her next words. "M-my name? My parents?"

"No, just you."

"From whom?"

"Not from me. I would never. Before Goody Stanford's trial, he did question a few girls your age."

Constance glanced up. She could see Sarah pursing her lips. She looked a little like Mrs. O'Conner, but less wrinkly. "I bet I know who. I knew Rose was mad at me, but to give my name?"

"I'm supposed to bring you in tomorrow. My master has ordered it."

Sara walked a few steps away, her arms around herself. "Then…that is what you have to do. It's your duty."

"I won't. I can't. You don't know what Reverend Michael does to these witches behind closed doors."

"And do you think I'm a witch?"

There was a pause. "I don't know. I just know that since the day I met you, I can't get you out of my head. I would do anything for you. And I can't let you get hurt. I've never felt this way before. I feel like I'm under some sort of spell."

Constance squirmed, feeling uncomfortable. They were saying a lot of words that often made people angry or afraid. But when Sarah laughed, she relaxed.

"I must be under the same spell, because the same thing has been happening to me."

They held hands.

"Then you need to leave, get as far away from New Hope as you can."

"Where? For how long? My parents can't leave; we don't have the money."

"You have to leave."

"To live in the woods? For who knows how long? I'd rather face the witch-hunter. I am strong. I will survive. I can last a few weeks in jail or three days in the stocks. I don't care as long as I can stay here with you."

"Sarah, you can't. People have died. I've seen it in Boston. Nobody has been sentenced here yet, but Reverend Michael isn't afraid to do it. I need you to leave."

"And then what? I come back to New Hope when this entire hullabaloo is over. Reverend Michael will be gone and you with him. You off to someplace new to learn to be a witch-hunter."

The silence lasted so long, Constance looked up to see if they had gone. Odin clawed at the tree as if it were a monster.

"We'll leave together. Tonight."

"What?"

"We'll run away. We'll go somewhere, anywhere. Boston. Philadelphia. New Amsterdam. Wherever you want to go. Reverend Michael won't follow us."

"I…I don't know."

"Isn't this what you wanted? To leave this town and go to a big city? Or is it that you don't want to go with me?"

"It's not that…It's just so sudden…I…I want to go, but not just because I'm running away. I would go with you even if you had asked me yesterday." She threw herself into the apprentice's arms.

They were hugging and whispering of plans in such low voices that not even Constance could hear. Then they departed, leaving the girl with the two cats. Not long after, Sarah returned.

"Constance, I need you to do something for me, sweetie," Sarah coaxed, placing a stiff paper in her hands. "This is a letter that I need you to give my parents."

Constance started to stand.

"No, not now, sweetie. Give it to them tomorrow," Sarah informed. "Do you understand? Tomorrow?"

Constance nodded without looking up. She liked to nod or shake her head. She wished that everyone would ask her only yes or no questions; it was simpler to communicate with gestures.

"Thank you, sweetie." Sarah kissed her crown, but that was all the contact she made. "I'm going away, and I'm taking Odin. We'll both miss you. Goodbye."

Misunderstanding, Constance took that as the sign that she was to go home. She stood up, letter in hand, and followed her usual path home, Lucifer sauntering after. Unbeknownst to her, the events following the disappearance of Sarah and the apprentice would eventually send her path careening into the witch-hunter's.

*   *   *

The departure of Sarah O'Conner and the witch-hunter's apprentice didn't go unnoticed. In light of the situation, the people of New Hope were eager for something else to gossip about. For days after, theories flew from one mouth to another, speculating on what had happened, the most popular that they had eloped. For those in the jail cells and inline to go in front of Reverend Michael, this bit of juicy news lessened their tribulations. Unfortunately, the only witness could not be pumped for information. Constance remained tight-lipped, even refusing to recite scripture.

For Reverend Michael, the loss of an apprentice was merely a bump on the nose of a witch. The life of a witch-hunter wasn't for everyone.[72] He'd had apprentices run off before for one reason or another, but this was the first that coincided with a witch escaping from justice. The boy had always been sloppy, even a bit too trusting, which was how that witch ensnared him.

While the lack of an apprentice was an

---

[72] Sometimes, it wasn't even for witch-hunters.

annoyance, the thought of another witch escaping the Lord's vengeance was another twist on the proverbial thumb screw.[73] First, Thou-Will's trickery, then Goody Stanford wriggling from his grasp, and now this Sarah O'Conner. These witches were making a fool of him.

"Thomas Biddle," Reverend Michael called, using the same tone when summoning his apprentice. When the round merchant entered the courtroom—which is where the witch-hunter did all his work, even drawing up papers—he explained, "With our cause being short-handed, I am promoting you to assistant witch-hunter. I have a letter here that needs to be dispersed to all the towns and cities nearby to spread word of a manhunt."

"For Goody Stanford?"

"No, for Sarah O'Conner and my apprentice. If we are quick, we may be able to save the boy from the witch's influence."

"You don't think they eloped?"

"Why would they?[74] No, it is my expertise that the witch found out that I suspected and fled before she could be seized. She most likely enchanted my apprentice, turning him into her slave for her twisted, seductive purposes[75] so she may move about freely."

---

[73] Which the reverend knew from first-hand knowledge just how painful that could be on another person.

[74] The reverend was skeptical of anyone who wanted to get married. Using paper and ink to keep two people together almost sounded like witchcraft to him, no matter what the church thinks of it.

[75] In a way, he was correct.

"Er…isn't that the same as elopement?" Thomas Biddle joked.

The reverend wouldn't know.

"It is of utmost importance that the letter be sent out. Can I trust you?"

"Of course, reverend. You know you can count on me. We have been partners almost from the start. I could never let one of my best customers down."

The reverend gave Thomas Biddle one of the rarest things he had: a smile, which was withered and meaningless.

"I am glad to have you. I will confide in you that I am…afraid for New Hope. I hadn't suspected that this infection had spread so deeply. It's almost as if…anyone could be a witch." He said this as if he found out an immoveable truth had become a lie.

"Maybe. Maybe," Thomas Biddle said, his voice mulling. "Perhaps, you should take it easy. You're workin' too hard. Maybe find a few more men to help out."

Reverend Michael nodded but didn't speak. It was sound advice, but moot. Nobody wanted to be responsible for arresting neighbors and friends for witchcraft He waved his assistant away. The crowds were starting to gather for the next witch trial. There was so much more to do, and he had no time to converse about his worries.

*   *   *

With no apprentice, Thomas Biddle became the transcriber for the trial that day. As a businessman, he had some education with his letters and numbers, but found the work below him. He suffered through the process, using ink blots in place of words he couldn't spell.

In the trial, the woman, a spinster with a wandering eye—or as the witch-hunter spun it, an evil eye—confessed only after ten minutes with the witch-hunter and his box. The crowd was disappointed; they did so love the lacquered box in action, but it was for the best. With the apprentice gone, it would be up to Biddle to clean up any mess left over from the torture. Reverend Michael insisted the courtroom be scrubbed spotless after each trial.[76]

After the trial, Biddle went to his store, dismissed his clerks, cleaned up, and emptied the safe before closing up. He went slowly, casually, stopping by his neighbor's home, whose wife he paid to do his laundry and cook him dinner every night. He lingered, catching up on the family and exchanging pleasantries before heading home. While he looked and acted natural, as if tomorrow would be just another day, inside he was a klaxon, screaming and panicking as if he were in the middle of the ocean and he had just set the sail on fire.

The witch-hunter may have just been talking, but his words were a warning signal. He could suspect anyone as a witch. Biddle had seen too much of Reverend Michael's methods to feel safe remaining in New Hope another day.

At that town meeting so many weeks ago, Biddle had formed a plan to cozy up to the witch-hunter and become his right-hand man. After years of heavy-

---

[76] Cleanliness is next to godliness.

dealing, unsavory money-lending and cooking the books by changing ones into sevens and threes into eights, all in his favor, he had made plenty of enemies. Eventually, someone would shout out his name in the confession box.

After speaking with the witch-hunter that morning, he knew everything was unraveling.
He may be jumping the gun, but he couldn't risk it. And he certainly couldn't haphazard the witch-hunter searching his house and finding his secret collection of occult items he treasured. Because Thomas Biddle was actually a witch. A big one.

One look at the books made of human skin, the statues of dark gods, and alters to a goat-headed creature, he wouldn't be allowed to just confess his sins, name a few names, and be given a slap on the wrist. It would be the gallows for him.

When Goody Stanford had announced she knew that there was a black witch in New Hope, he had held his breath, waiting for her to say his name. It had been a relief that she didn't know it was him that had created the talisman and brought mice from miles around to eat every last bit of the harvest and food while he had stock piled mouse-proof containers with grain, dried fruits and other foodstuffs in anticipation of raising his prices and taking advantage of the "disaster."

It hadn't been his first spell. He had performed small charms and curses, giving people he disliked a little bad luck, and helping his business with good luck. The mice plague had been his coup de grâce. But it had all backfired on him, bringing the witch-hunter to New Hope and forcing him to flee for his life.

Waiting until dark, he packed up what wealth he could with a few supplies and saddled his horse. Even though he was a worldly man, he had no worldly attachments to the store, his house, or any of the people. There was only one thing he was so attached to that he couldn't live without: himself.

As for the letter that he promised to send out with a currier, he had ripped it up and thrown it out with the hopes that the witch-hunter would be so distracted by his apprentice's disappearance, it would give Biddle a few days to escape, becoming anonymous in the world. But where?

Boston was crawling with wiccaphobes and hunters, the craze sprawled all over the coast. No, what he needed was somewhere nobody would think he would go, a city nobody had even heard of. A place where the word "witch" wasn't part of everyday conversation.

He had heard that Salem was nice this time of year.

*   *   *

Between the growing list of names and searching for Goody Stanford, Sarah O'Conner, and his apprentice, Reverend Michael had been too busy to notice that Thomas Biddle didn't come to work the next day. By this time, Phinchas Partridge had ten cells built.

After going through three more witch trials and hearing no news on the manhunt, Reverend Michael felt the empty hole that Thomas Biddle had filled, realizing he had not seen the man in several days. It didn't take long for him to march to the general store owner's houses. He feared the worse, that a witch had killed him.

The truth was more painful.

After finding out that a man he believed understood his mandate of hunting down witches, who had worked so closely to him, was a witch, Reverend Michael realized he had been too soft on these witches. He could no longer afford to go at the pace he was going lest he be tricked or betrayed once again.

So, he trusted no one. He sent a messenger to the nearest town to hire help, four toughs that hadn't been corrupted by New Hope, using Thomas Biddle's forsaken wares to pay their wages.[77]

By this time, the humble hamlet of New Hope had accepted the underlying truth of what witch-hunting was about; it was only business. Word spread on the protocol of what happened when accused.

Let the fourth wall crack for a moment and imagine that it is you that will be accused of witchcraft. First, there would be a lot of yelling, screaming, and finger-pointing as neighbors and friends lie in great detail how you, as a witch, have cast nasty spells that cause ague and rheumatism in their joints as well as keeping the baby up all night and little Elizabeth to fall and skin her knee. Now,

---

[77] A witch's property was often seized. What a coincidence that when the public finally figured this out, the fabulously wealthy became fabulously witch-like.

you could deny it, but nobody would believe you. It is now a fact that you are a witch, and there is nothing you can do about it.

The law says that all witches must be hanged, that is, unless you confess your sins and name any accomplices. And everyone knows, witches always have accomplices. So, you have the choice of dying or accepting this inarguable truth, confess, and give up a few names, any names. It may help your cause if you allow the reverend to perform some light torture on you, maybe a little thumb-screwing, a few picks, scream at the top of your lungs. He may even give you a lighter sentence.

After all, a little pain is a vacation compared to hanging.

Once your interrogation is over, you'll share a nice, cozy cell for a few weeks or you can stand in the stocks for three days without food and water while the whole town points and laughs at you, throwing rotten food, rocks, whatever is handy. Sounds like a breeze, doesn't it?

But there is really nothing you can do; you just have to ride it out in this order.

Which is exactly what every citizen of New Hope had either gone through or looked forward to each day, no telling when their name would be whispered in the ear of Reverend Michael.

From the moment that he found out about Biddle's betrayal, Reverend Michael became a different man. It was him and God against the world. He vowed never to allow a witch to get the best of him, again.

Being outsmarted three times, Reverend Michael was convinced that a head witch lived in New Hope, but he would no longer allow this hell-bride to get away with her evil deeds. There was a tactic that was handed down from one witch-hunter to the next, a fail-safe of finding the head witch. For the plan to work, he needed a cooperative witch, one who was willing to do unspeakable things to save their lives. Some witches would prefer to hang than to stoop so low as to cooperate in such a despicable plan.

It was time to make a witch's cake.

*   *   *

Reverend Michael was never one to play favorites, even when donations[78] were involved. However, he was known to play dis-favorites. Sometimes, out of a twisted sense of honor, disreputable men would be named in interrogation just to get them off the streets. Most of the time, these men—drunks, tramps, wanderers, madmen—were innocent. So, to save on time, the reverend often left these men alone, knowing it was a dead-end. These types of men didn't even know their own names much less any witches.

However, Reverend Michael was getting a sense that if he swung a dead cat by its tail in New Hope, he'd hit a witch. Nobody had led him wrong so far. When preparing the witch's cake, he selected Gilly to be his witch.

Everyone and their dog had given up Gilly's

---

[78]*cough* bribes *cough*

name because he was a drunk. Where he attained drinks, nobody knew since he had no profession, no source of income, and lived in a dingy shack behind the butcher. Somehow, he had achieved the mental prowess to persuade the frequent patrons of the pubs that it was a service to buy him a drink while at the same time being completely unaware of anything else happening around him. He could find alcohol in a desert, and go without a drink for hours and still be tipsy. The man had veins of beer.

Of course, due to the sensitive nature of this interrogation, Gilly's trial took place in absolute secrecy in the dead of night without a transcriptor to record even a single cough.

The minute Reverend Michael's hired thug set the disheveled, smelly drunk on the chair, Gilly screamed, "I swears, I didn't do it."

"What didn't you do?" Reverend Michael asked patiently. Men of Gilly's nature tended to speak freely in any situation.

"Whatever it is you think I did," Gilly replied, red-veined eyes wandering the courthouse in loops. "Nice place ya got here."

The witch-hunter sighed. "Can I get you a drink?" he asked, playing the role of good witch-hunter.

"I ain't never touched the stuff. I'm a good Christian," Gilly said with a hiccup.

"I was offering water."

"What year?"

Reverend Michael paused. *So, it's going to be like that…*

"Mr. Gilly, let us cut to—"

"Who?"

"I'm referring to you."

"My name ain't Mister."

"Gilly, then."

"An' don't you forget it." He raised his hand as if it were habit to take a drink as this time and looked confused as to why he wasn't holding anything.

"Gilly, you are accused of being a witch."

"I told you, I didn't do it. An' that woman never saw me do it neither," Gilly insisted.

"Do what?"

"The thing she didn't see me do."

"What woman?"

"The woman that t'wert there."

"She saw you performing witchcraft?"

"Witchcraft? Naw, I can't. I don't own a toad."

The reverend massaged the bridge of his nose. "The absence of amphibious creatures isn't vindication. I have witnesses that have seen your name in the Devil's book and performing dark arts. Is this true?"

"As long as you ain't accusin' me of…that other thing that I didn't do, then witchcrafts isn't so bad, eh?"

"The penalty for witchcraft is death."

Gilly shook his head. "No, no, I ain't pleadin' guilty to bein' a witch. I'll say I did that other thing. What's the punishment for that?"

"For what?"

"For that thing I didn't do."

"I didn't bring you here for some petty crime, whatever it is. I have no knowledge of that."

"Then we're done here," Gilly stated, standing.

One of the hired hands, a man who was built like a sack of potatoes that spent its time lifting weights on the beach, pushed the drunk back down.

"You aren't leaving until either I get a confession or you prove that you aren't a witch."

"I can prove that. I can't be a witch on account that I ain't a woman."

"Men can be witches," Reverend Michael argued, his voice rising in volume.

"No, I heard somewhere about all witches are women." Gilly paused. "Or is it all women are witches.[79] Never mind, I think you're right. Carry on."

"So, will you confess?"

"I didn't do it. An' that woman can't prove it. She saw nothin' because she wasn't there."

"Are you a witch?" the reverend shouted. Usually he shouted because he wanted to, but this asinine conversation set him to yelling involuntarily.

"No!"

"Then what do you call this?" The witch-hunter grabbed Gilly's hand, showing a brown mark. This time, he made sure it wasn't dried stew.

"It's a mark."

"Given to you by the Devil."

"It is?" Gilly looked at the mark with renewed interest.

"This is proof that you are a witch."

Gilly's eyes dazzled at this revelation. "I must be."

Victory at last. The reverend didn't take any

---

[79] The same is true for snitches, rhymes included.

pleasure in besting a drunk, but a victory nonetheless. Which brought him to his ulterior motive.

"With your confession, normally, I would require the names of your fellow witches, but I am giving you a unique opportunity to complete your repentance back to God."

"To God? Does this mean I go to the gallows?"

"Not if you aid us. There's a way to find a powerful witch, the head witch of New Hope, but we need your aid."

"Sound like a plan. What do I do?"

"I need something from you."

"Sorry, I'm a bit short on money. Which reminds me, could you lend me a few coins for…something I need? It ain't liquor."

"Gilly, do you know what a witch's cake is?"

"Is it like a witch's pie?"

"To make a witch's cake, I need an ingredient that only a witch can provide. I need you to fill that bucket." The reverend pointed to a metal bucket in the corner. It was obviously a well-used facility of the jail by the smell.

Gilly looked at the pail with suspicion. "Hey, I thought you said that you didn't know about that thing that I said that I didn't do."

Raising one eyebrow a fraction, the reverend had an inkling as to what minor infraction Gilly kept professing his innocence. "Fill the bucket."

"Well, alright. But only 'cause I like you. It's a good thing I'm ready to make this witch's cake. I've been drinkin'…water all day." He tried to look innocent as he moved to the corner and unbuckled his pants.

After the bucket sloshed with the gifted ingredient, Reverend Michael and Gilly watched as one of the thugs, this one built more like a brick wall on steroids, made a witch's cake.[80] With the cake created, the first thug brought in one of Faithful Goodman's cats that had been shanghaied after weeks of careful stalking.

Her name was Pookey.

Dumped unceremoniously out of the sack onto the table, Pookey clawed and hissed at her captors before turning her attention to the dubious, moist lump the consistency of vomited oatmeal. As cats are prone to do with grotesque items, she sniffed it.

Cats have tastes that can lean one way or another drastically. They might turn their noses up at the fanciest meals while gobbling garbage down then cough it up later at a more convenient time.[81] Yet one whiff of the witch's cake was all Pookey needed to sneeze her distaste.

"Cat, I command you to eat that witch's cake," the reverend ordered.

In reply, Pookey cleaned underneath her tail, showing the clergyman that although she may lick her own butt, she would refuse to eat the cake.

Reverend Michael spoke to the two hired thugs he had in the room. "Force it down its throat."

The thugs exchanged looks which would be similar to two male gorillas acknowledging each other. Then one spoke with the tone of one with an IQ

---

[80] A process just as disgusting as anyone can imagine based on what little information has been mentioned.

[81] Like on an expensive rug or when dinner guests are over.

lower than room temperature in a mountain cabin in winter. "We don't do cats."

"What do you mean?" Reverend Michael asked, offended. He was surprised that the men could even speak.

"Wells, that weren't part o' the job descript-yon."

"Your job is whatever I require. And I require you to make this cat eat that witch's cake."

"Yous ne'er say anythin' abou' cruelty ta annymals."

"You told me you had no problem with torture and other interrogation measures." Reverend Michael gritted his teeth. When he hired the men, he had looked for ones with small heads with big muscles. Apparently, even that size ratio came with their own problems.

"That's people. Nothin' wrong wit' hurtin' people. Rob, here, is pacifically soft-hearted 'wards annymals. Says they's better than people."

Pookey smiled the way cats smile when they hear inarguable and flattering truth.

"Annymals are in-hair-iently good."

The silent Rob, nodded, as if he signed a contract backing up his partner's words.

Reverend Michael opened his mouth, but Gilly spoke first.

"Well, what if this cat ain't all that good?"

The gorilla frowned, as if someone had just told him the sky was purple. "Wot?"

"Some cats aren't all that good. What if this one ain't?" Gilly asked. "What if it likes to kill songbirds for fun and makin' witch's cakes in people's shoes?"

Pookey's smile deepened proudly.

The two gorillas exchanged different looks as if having a silent argument.

"Don't matter. Still ain't doin' it."

Reverend Michael tried for a loop hole. "What about witch familiars? Are you soft-hearted towards them?"

"What are witches familiar wit'?"

Massaging his temples, the witch-hunter explained, "Witch familiars are demons that take the shape of animals to help witches with their evil deeds. Would you be fine with cruelty towards them?"

Again, the bulky men quietly conversed with eyebrows.

"Rob says that's fine."

It took both of them to wrestle the cat, pry her jaws open, and push in the noxious concoction.[82] To say the least, the thugs came out the worst off.

Freed, the cat jumped off the table and ran into the corner, puffed up and hissing. She scratched at the door, then glared at the men.

"What's the cake supposed to do?" Gilly asked, watching the cat as if she were the most interesting thing he had ever seen.

"It will cause the demon to speak the name of the head witch."

"It'll talk? How long will it take?"

"Not long."

"If it doesn't talk, do I still get to leave?"

"Quiet. It's doing something."

Pookey worked her jaws in a strange way before

---

[82] Anyone who has been ruthlessly prescribed by a vet to give their beloved cat a pill can sympathize with these men.

looking at the humans and uttering a word. "Meow."

"Heavens, did you hear that? It spoke," Gilly exclaimed, jumping up and down like a child. "I didn't think it would work. That's amazin'. Hey, are you a witch or somethin'?"[83]

That's when the cat retched up the witch's cake before staring at the hired assistants as if saying, "What are you waiting for? Clean that up."

"What are you waiting for? Clean that up," the reverend ordered his employees. He then grabbed Gilly by the collar and slammed him into a wall. "As for you, you're going to give me a name. One name, or it's to the gallows for you."

Gilly straightened, his eyes clearing. He hadn't been sober in ten years, but he was in that moment. He gave the only name he could think of: the woman who wasn't there to see the thing that he didn't do.

The magistrate's wife.

*　　　　*　　　　*

Even in this time when neighbors and friends turned against each other, there had been a line that everyone knew shouldn't be crossed. There were some people you just didn't accuse as a witch. Gilly had not only stepped over that line, he set it on fire, taken the ashes, put them in a sack, and threw it into the river.

Once the witch-hunter brought in the

---

[83]Gilly hit the nail on the head. Ironically, this particular witch-hunting technic is so close to witchcraft, many witch-hunters had put themselves on trial for it.

magistrate's wife to be questioned, all bets were off. Nobody could hide behind money, power, or position. Soon after that, age wasn't a factor either. It wasn't long before children became the popular witch demographic.

Besides those of the Partridge family, James Quinton was the next to be brought before Reverend Michael. It may surprise some that a child of only eight years could be thought of as a witch, but a mind could easily be swayed after meeting James. He wasn't well-liked for reasons. He kicked dogs, pulled the legs off of grasshoppers, and threw rocks at birds. Many truly believed that he was a witch soon after hearing the news.[84]

As smug as a child who could insult adults with the knowledge that they couldn't do anything in return, James bantered with the reverend before naming several boys and girls that he disliked immensely. That smugness retreated once Reverend Michael proclaimed a substitute sentence for all youth: a good beating.

One by one, the youth of New Hope were brought to trial, each one given an easy chance to repent with penance meaning a sore backside. After all, if a witch-hunter wanted to keep the support of the people, he didn't make tiny examples out of tiny people.

Meredith Longsdale, five years of age, didn't want to be the exception. As the days passed by, she watched as her peers were taken away one-by-one, enviously.

---

[84] He wasn't really, just a horrible child.

Each time one of the children returned from talking to "The Black Reverend" as they called the witch-hunter, they would swagger and brag about how they stood up against hours of questioning and torture. Each story was grander than the next, a soliloquy of boasting and bravery.

Meredith couldn't wait until it was her turn. But everyone said she was too young. She hated that, as if she was a baby, that she couldn't be brave. She even asked some of the older children to give up her name.

"Why would I do that? I'm not going to admit to being a witch. I'm standing up to the Black Reverend," they would tell her, scoffing at her attempts. And when they returned, named a witch after receiving their dozen or so switches, she would ask if they gave up her name. "How would that look if I gave the name of practically a baby? The Black Reverend would think I was a coward."

Then one day, as the older children were recounting their stories, she broke in, "I'd outlast all of you. The Black Reverend doesn't frighten me."

The next day, she and her parents were escorted to the witch-hunter.

Most trials involving children were closed to the public. Meredith wished it wasn't; she wanted all the older children to watch her stare down the Black Reverend. Although she had never been to a trial, she had heard enough snippets from eavesdropping and the other children to have an idea. But secondhand knowledge comes at a dangerous price, for she thought of the trials much like she would a ghost story; they were exciting and scary, but harmless.

Her parents looked nervous, and her mother was crying not at all silently. It was embarrassing how cowardly they were when she was giving the Black Reverend such a valiant show.

"Meredith Longsdale, you are accused of witchcraft. How do you plead?" the Black Reverend spoke in a voice that could rust a plow.

"I'm no witch," Meredith committed with head high.

Her mother cried harder.

"She doesn't know what she's saying, Reverend Michael," her father groveled. "She pleads guilty, of course. She's a witch, just like we are…were."

The witch-hunter's face twitched; for a moment, he looked like a mad dog before his face resumed the stoic stone.

"Daddy, I'm not a witch," Meredith said, disgusted that he would cave in. How could he admit to performing witchcraft, admitting to such a dark deed? After all these years of dragging her to church, lecturing her about God's laws and commandments, and punishing her for small sins, how could he confess to such a dark thing? Well, she wasn't so weak.

"I'm not a witch," Meredith proclaimed, looking the Black Reverend in his cold, green eyes. "And I'll never say I am." She meant it as a challenge.

"You're crimes have already been called in more than once," the Black Reverend spoke with fingers steepled. "I may have believed their words as black lies to destroy an innocent child because of your young age, but it wasn't just two or three witches but many. I cannot ignore the evidence."

Meredith's heart quickened. Many of the other children had named her, but they all told her that they didn't. Who was it?

"Please don't do this," her mother wailed.

The Black Reverend nodded in understanding. "The crimes of the children are often the fault of the parents. It was your dabbling in the dark arts that left her susceptible to the Devil's influence."

Meredith's anger took over. Why didn't they listen to her? "I'm not a witch," she shouted. Then she threw in for good measure, "And you can't make me say that I am." It was a line she borrowed from a ten-year-old boy's retellings of his own trial, so it must be the right thing to say.

The Black Reverend's eyebrows lifted, his head nodding slightly as if he finally understood. "Very well." He moved away from the table and reached for a lacquered box.

Meredith's mother broke out in fresh, louder cries, turning to Meredith's father for comfort.

"No, please. She's too young."

"If she is not too young to flout such words to a man of God, then she is not too young to understand that her soul is teetering on the edge of damnation. You have repented of your own transgressions, but you failed to bring your daughter back to the light, and that may be unforgiveable," the Black Reverend snapped, his words as rapid as gunfire. He opened his box. "If you do not want to pull your child back into God's embrace, then allow me to do what you can't, that is if you are truly repentant of your sins."

Meredith's parents opened their mouths to protest, but nothing came out. Their fear was evident.

Meredith couldn't believe how they laid down and allowed themselves to be bad mouthed by the preacher. She had heard many of the children criticize the adults for succumbing to the Black Reverend's words, which was why she naively condemned them with her eyes before turning to the witch-hunter, eager to show him her metal.

The Black Reverend opened the box, the hinges squeaking slightly. He said nothing; something Meredith hadn't expected. She had imagined questions being thrown here and there, great debates and screaming, all of which she had prepared herself for. She even readied herself for torture, a word she associated with boys pulling hair and pinching, all of which she had endured her whole life. But she didn't think that there would be so much silence, nor did she really think about the legendary, lacquered box.

She knew about the box only from the words of others, and usually with as little detail as possible. Her heart quickened at the sleek wood, the flash of metal and the dark velvet lining. Finally, this was the moment she had waited for; this was her test.

As the reverend pulled out the first iron instrument, her knees grew weak. The second one, she was biting her lip. The third, she was rethinking her strategy. She inspected the items, not because she was curious, but because her fear refused to let her look away. These weren't knives made for cooking, chopping, and slicing, but fine, delicate tools that were made to squeeze out as much pain with as little effort.

By the time the box was empty, Meredith was crying, her imagination giving her an idea of what was in store for her. When the Black Reverend picked up a knife with a smooth, gentle arch, she had to clench her knees together. At the age of five, she still had problems with her bladder, and at that moment, she could feel her body giving in to her fear.

"Please," she cried out. "I-I didn't mean it. I just wanted to be brave like all the others. Don't hurt me, please."

The Black Reverend didn't lower the knife. "There is only one thing that will save you today, my child."

Meredith sobbed.

"Are you a witch?"

Meredith saw her parents silently bob their heads, helping her to choose an answer.

To this, Meredith nodded in return. All her life, she had been told how bad lying was. She still didn't understand the situation, but had a twisted idea that for some reason, the Black Reverend had come just to see how many people he could get to lie. It wasn't until this moment that she knew what had caused the adults to break such a sacred commandment.

She knew she had to sin to save herself.

"Yes, I'm a witch," she sobbed, feeling relieved when the Black Reverend lowered the scalpel.

"Give me the names of the other witches that you know," the Black Reverend ordered. He may have lowered the knife, but his hand still caressed it.

Meredith wanted to look at the man's eyes, but they were locked on the knife, thinking of it scraping away her skin, nerves, and blood. Within seconds, her parents were at her side.

"Just give him the name of a witch, honey," her father whispered. "Any name will do. He doesn't need more than that. He'll understand with your age."

Her mother murmured encouragement. "Just say any name. It could be anyone."

She wanted to say a name. She wanted to so badly, but her eyes were sealed on all those destructive metal instruments, her imagination painting blood all over them, her blood. She couldn't say anything. Her mouth wouldn't move.

The witch-hunter rolled a needle across the table.

Meredith yelped and hopped in her chair as if she had been pricked. "Constance!" she shouted, relieved to have said something. But as her ears heard the name, she felt worse than before. Her stomach churned, hot and acidy, her breath burning her throat. She would allow the Black Reverend to poke and stab her with all his torture devices if she could take that name back.

"Constance?"

"Constance Sanderson. She's an orphan, a girl who is not of her entire faculties. My daughter is frightened and said the first name she thought of. She didn't mean it."

Meredith nodded. She really didn't. There were other names she could have said. Why did she give Constance's name?

"From out of the mouths of babes," the Black Reverend said, a cold, calculating smile on his face. "Your daughter knew what she was doing for she was being guided by God."

"No, I lied," Meredith shouted, her tongue returned. "I didn't mean to say her name. She's not a witch, honest."

"I cannot believe you. In fact, by the way you are protesting, I have to wonder if you're intentions are noble. The Devil may be directing you, to preserve his most faithful of followers."

"But Constance is…she's not smart. She's the least likely to be a witch in all of New Hope," Meredith's mother protested. "Have you not met the child? She can't speak her own words. She acts more like a baby. You must be mistaken."

"And sometimes the servants of darkness use deception to fool those around them."

Meredith and her parents protested again, but the Black Reverend waved his hand in dismissal.

"That is enough. I need no more from your daughter. She'll receive ten strikes of the whip for punishment for her transgressions, which my assistant will administer on your way out. And make sure she doesn't commune with devils again."

Meredith took the punishment gladly, accepting the pain to her rump as penalty for bringing Constance to the Black Reverend's attention.

She rationalize that all Constance had to do was admit to being a witch and then give someone else's name, a simple thing, really. It was a shame that Constance would have to be whipped as well, but as long as she did just as Meredith had done, she'd be fine. If Meredith, a little five-year-old, could do it, thirteen-year-old Constance could as well.

Nobody would have to know it was Meredith who gave the Black Reverend her name. She knew of two other children who had seen the Black Reverend that same day, any of them could have given up Constance. She was in the clear.

The next day, save for an aching bottom, she returned to her usual play. Part of her even accepted the lie as truth, her perception of witches now consisting of liars. She was glad she was a witch. All her friends were witches, her parents were witches. A strange pride filled her. She was the youngest witch in town.

As the older children gathered to tell their stories of the Black Reverend, she proudly announced she had been in with the witch-hunter. Many denied this, but when she described the lacquered box and all the knives and pointy things, the others nodded.

"How long did you last under torture?" her friend Ann asked.

She looked up into the faces of the older children, some as big as ten years. She didn't want to admit to them that she didn't even last one minute. But she saw something she hadn't noticed before. As she described the lacquered box and the instruments of torture, she saw pale cheeks and fearful eyes. Their boasting had stopped, and she understood them as if she could read their minds.

They had all lied about their time with the witch-hunter. She knew this as truth just as she knew her own name.

"I don't remember," she said, imitating the boastful voices the others had used. "It must have been at least two hours. Maybe three."

She continued bragging, but whenever she made eye-contact with the other children, those who had been in with the Black Reverend, they shared a wordless agreement that the truth would never be revealed.

That they were all afraid of the Black Reverend.

*   *   *

If Constance's name had come up sooner, perhaps someone could have done something about it. A persuasive word or a stern lecture that Reverend Michael may have gone too far may have stopped what came next, but the witch-hunter was like a rolling stone, building in momentum. His cause was too big; he had too much power.

Not to mention, he had been waiting for this moment. He hadn't known it was a moment until Meredith had given up the girl's name. New Hope was more than he had dreamed it could be with an abundance of witches *and* a head witch. He at first thought it was Goody Stanford, but her name had been given up too easily, and she had little influence in the town. Then he thought it was someone of influence, perhaps the magistrate or his wife, but both of them caved in too easily.

Then he considered something the instant Meredith spoke the name. His hypothesis cemented more and more with each protest. Could it be? Could he really have found the head witch?

Constance, a girl nobody would notice, a person who always seemed to be in the background. Her behavior, how she never made eye-contact, how she traced spells with her fingers in the dirt, and how she muttered nonsense to herself, while strange, was textbook demon-style.

She was the head witch, she had to be.

But he couldn't let her know that he had found out. If she knew, then there would be great trouble. So, when he brought her in for a trial—closed to the public, of course—he acted as if this were an ordinary interrogation. He began with the usual questions, building in intensity.

Unlike everyone else in the town, she didn't say anything, merely flinched when he yelled. Anyone her age would try to act like an adult in this situation, but she behaved more like an animal. She rocked in her chair, arms crossed over her chest protectively. At times, she even curled up into a ball, moaning.

Her cat, the feral, unkempt beast that couldn't be removed from the courtroom once he slid in, had kept up a discordant melody the entire time. The thing was a constant pest, always close to the child but also always out of reach.

At one particular moment, Reverend Michael pounded on the table to emphasis his question, which sent Constance into a shrieking mess as she covered her ears.

"Stop it. You're scaring her," Constance's aunt pleaded, holding her niece and stroking her hair. "She's innocent. Let her go."

The reverend glared at the woman, irritated by her interference. At this point, most parents helped rather than hindered by persuading their little ones to cooperate. But this couple wasted energy trying to convince him of the girl's innocence. Their staunchness only galvanized his belief of who Constance really was.

Constance's uncle stood against the reverend like they were equals. "Don't you understand her condition? She's touched in the head, born that way. Can't you see she has no idea of what you are asking her?"

The cat yowled as if to second this.

"Silence," Reverend Michael growled more to the cat than the uncle. Its pitch had increased in irritating magnitude the past ten minutes. "As reformed witches, you have no business in interfering with the work of God. If you continue to prevent me from saving your niece's soul, then I might suspect that your earlier repentance was a farce."

"No, it wasn't. We have repented," the woman proclaimed.

Constance's uncle, who had been a preacher until his congregation stopped coming to his church, didn't say anything, either out of anger or shame.

"Then stop your coddling. If the child is to be redeemed, then you must let me work." The reverend remembered how the other children confessed quickly at the sight of his box. If she is like a child as others claimed, then it would work on her as well.

But when the lid of the box creaked open, Constance didn't even look up. Instead, she had her knees up to her chin, rocking and muttering. No, she was reciting. What was she saying?

When he raised The Wrath of God, again the aunt and uncle protested; the cat hissed.

"Stop. She's just a child," the aunt screamed.

"She's a named witch. She'll either confess, or I'll make sure, as God is my witness, that she's as innocent as you say. I will be steadfast," the witch-hunter swore, invoking one of his names.

Understanding, the aunt grabbed her husband's hand. "We need to convince her."

Together, the knelt at Constance's side, speaking in soothing tones. "Sweetie, all you need to say is that you're a witch. That's it, and we can go home."

Constance shook her head violently. "'Thou shalt not bear false witness against thy neighbor,'" she quoted quietly.

"Say it," her uncle ordered, shaking her shoulders. "Just this once, listen to me and do as you're told."

"It's a game," the aunt cajoled. "You like games. If you say those words, then you win."

"'Let the lying lips be put to silence; which speak grievous things proudly and contemptuously against the righteous,'" Constance spoke louder.

"Clever witch, using the Lord's words to her advantage," Reverend Michael muttered.

"Isn't this proof of her innocence? A witch wouldn't know the scriptures like she does," the aunt argued.

"It is convincing, but it won't save her. No, a witch of her caliber could even repeat the Lord's prayer without flinching."

They looked at him in a way he hated, like as if he had said something that was vile and wicked. How dare they look at him that way? How dare they judge him as if they were on the right hand of God?

"You're a fool," the uncle shouted vehemently. "Don't you understand? She's not a witch. I'm not a witch. None of us are. We confessed because it was easy and we were afraid. But you won't stop, not when you're blinded by power and can't see that you're not doing any good. Nothing you've done has been in God's name."

One second, the witch-hunter stood as still as a mountain, the next he had the uncle's arm pinned to the table, The Wrath of God pinched between two fingers. As he shoved the metal under a fingernail, he asked over the man's screams, "Are you still afraid?"

The aunt sobbed hysterically, while the cat ran around the room like a maniac.

Over the cacophony, Constance's agitated voice recited, "'The Lord is my shepherd; I shall not want. He maketh me to lie down in green pastures; he leadeth me...'"

Like a stream diverted for irrigation, the reverend's attention pitched from the uncle to the girl, his face filled with wonder as he listened to chapter after chapter of Psalms. She didn't stop, only paused for breath. It was perfect. Emotionless. Inhuman.

Rage diminishing, he released his hold of the uncle. Pulling out a handkerchief, he meticulously cleaned The Wrath of God. It was clear to him that the witch was beyond any means to force a confession. Constance was different than the others.

"You may go," he told the aunt and uncle, the latter stanching blood flowing from his finger.

"We can?" the aunt asked, relieved. "Come on, Constance. Let's go."

"No, you and your husband can go. Constance is to remain in jail until her sentence."

"H-her sentence?" By the look of the woman's face, another bout of crying threatened to erupt.

"She refused to repent. As such, she'll suffer the consequences. The punishment for witchcraft is death by hanging."

Lucky for Reverend Michael, he had two hired thugs to drag the man and woman away before they could cause a scene. As for Constance, she meekly followed a third hired hand to the jailhouse, the scruffy cat shadowing her.

With the interrogation room quiet, the reverend looked back on his accomplishments. He had gone further than he thought. None of his other colleagues could compare to his achievements. So many wayward souls turned back to the light, so many witches confessed, and one to be eliminated.

"I will be steadfast."

*   *   *

The announcement of Constance's execution killed the town's good humor faster than a flashflood. New Hope didn't have a gallows, had no need of one. A simple tree branch would have done the job, but Reverend Michael demanded that the occasion called for something more to make a statement. He needed everyone in the crowd to see.

This was his greatest moment, his time to shine in front of the Lord.

The hired thugs, moonlighting as carpenters, built the gallows in the town square. Nobody could go anywhere without seeing the progress, the countdown to Constance's death. No more names were spoken. No more confessions were squeezed out in the courthouse. It was as if a holiday had been declared for the witch-hunter.

The reverend received letters from ministers, petitioning for Constance's life, but he would not be moved.

The magistrate argued if it was the best time to make an example of the thirteen-year-old girl, but the reverend would not be moved.

If his own mother dragged herself from her grave just to speak on the girl's behalf, he would not be moved.

He was Reverend Michael Be-Steadfast Fear-God Kill-Sin Boggust, and he would live up to his name.

The day rolled in with fog crowding the corners of New Hope as if to hide the execution from the world. The townsfolk were listless in their morning routine, accomplishing the bare minimum before heading to the town square.

Nobody wanted to go, but they did; it felt wrong to stay at home. They needed to go, not for any macabre curiosity, but out of respect for Constance.

As the clock chimed neatly at noon, the hired men marched Constance to the gallows where Reverend Michael waited, standing above the crowd, calm and serene with his hands behind his back. With his black clothes and thin frame, he could have been the Grim Reaper except without the charisma.

Constance whispered inaudibly as she walked through the crowd. She was still dressed in the same clothes from her interrogation, dirtier and thinner, and distant from reality. She didn't react when her guardians called out. Behind, Lucifer padded along, glad to be outside. He moved as if the crowd had gathered for him.

Knowing that the cat would be joining his mistress, Reverend Michael had a second noose set up and hoovering a foot above the platform in anticipation for a witch's familiar's neck.

The hired men hardly had to direct the girl up the stairs, her feet moving mechanically, her eyes cast down. She only stopped when the noose framed her face. Lucifer took his spot under his own rope, stretching to give it a sniff.

Reverend Michael opened the event with, "As the Book of Exodus states, 'Thou shalt not suffer a witch to live.' But it is also written that those who confess their sins shall be forgiven. Let us see the difference between those who are converted and those who are not." He expected to see enlightenment in the crowd, to see gratitude for freeing them from the power of Satan. But he only saw hollow gazes.

"'Inasmuch as ye have done it unto one of the least of these my brethren,'" Constance quoted in her distant voice, "'ye have done it unto me.'"

Glaring at the condemned witch, the reverend placed the noose roughly over the girl's neck. "Any last words, witch?"

Constance shrugged her shoulders at the chaffing noose. "'For the Lord seeth not as man seeth; for man looketh on the outward appearance, but the Lord looketh on the heart.'"

"And what of your heart? Will you finally confess?"

"'If a false witness rise up against any man to testify against him that which is wrong...'" Constance began.

As she recited, the witch-hunter recognized the verse, and it enraged him. He grabbed for his lacquered box, but it wasn't with him.

"'...then shall ye do unto him, as he had thought to have done unto his brother: so shalt thou put the evil away from among you.'"

"I am Reverend Michael Be-Steadfast Fear-God Kill-Sin Boggust," he growled. "I'm the avenging angel. I will be steadfast. I will kill sin. I remind others to fear God. I will not be moved."

The young girl, standing two heads shorter than the witch-hunter, looked him in the face for the first time, her eyes penetrating the curtain of her hair. They were green, but not like his. Hers were bright and clear, yet were unfocused as if seeing beyond him. "I am Constantly-Loves-God. I am His sheep, His follower. I will bow to His will."

"So be it," the reverend hissed, tightening the noose. Before he could address the crowd again and end the witch's life, the girl's voice caught his attention.

"Forgive me, Father, for I have sinned," she whispered.

It was a common phrase in his line of work, one he had been expecting for so long. It was about time she caved in and confessed.

"I believe that Thou hast forsaken me. Help Thou mine unbelief," she cried out, the first emotion he'd seen from her. Her eyes searched the crowd then widened as she pointed. "I see."

Curious, the reverend followed her finger. "Yes? What do you see?"

"A witch."

"A witch?"

"Yes."

"Who? Give me the name." He couldn't stop the anticipation in his voice, like a wolf creeping up on wayward sheep.

"Faithful Goodman."

The crowd, who had watched this interchange, turned to look at the elderly woman, who smiled congenially.

Disappointed, the reverend thumped the rail of the gallows. "I know that. I need a new name."

Constance's finger moved. "Edith Partridge. Thomas Partridge. Robert Partridge." She named the large woman and each of her nine children—save for the baby—before moving on, spouting name after name, her finger and tongue moving faster and faster.

She was reciting the names in the order they had been accused, perfectly. She hardly hesitated, finding them without error. Thou-Will, Gilly, her guardians, James Quincy, and ending with Meredith who had named Constance. Then, slowly, her finger moved up to the reverend, her green eyes piercing.

The crowd held a collective breath.

"Reverend Michael Be-Steadfast Kill-Sin Fear-God Boggust is not a witch," Constance stated.

The crowd exhaled, the air heavy with disappointment as if they expected something more climatic.

Constance's finger moved to the witch-hunter's hired men who lined the back of the gallows. "Not a witch. Not a witch. Not a witch. Not a witch."

The men exchanged looks of relief at this declaration. They knew first hand, literally, what happened to witches in this town.

"Five not-a witches in a town full of witches," Constance said, sounding pleased with her math.

Lucifer purred so loud, the gallows rumbled.

Nervousness fell on the hired men like a sudden shower.

The crowd looked around, realizing that they couldn't spit without hitting a confessed witch. Those few that hadn't yet come to the reverend's attention were drowned out by witches.

The reverend, with his advantageous view, saw the transformation of the crowd. It came in waves. First, confusion lapped at the shore, then a wave of thinking before comprehension finally crashed down. That's when Reverend Michael saw that he stood in the middle of, not a crowd, but a monster. A monster of his own creation. A monster who finally grasped that the person poking and prodding it was now a lot smaller than it.

Never had a mob found pitchforks and torches so quickly.

Constance remained on the gallows until her aunt and uncle could remove the noose and lead her down, Lucifer twining between their legs. There was no look of triumph, no relief, nothing to indicate what she had done. It was as if she had been possessed by something. And now, back to her old self, she recited to her aunt and uncle.

"'Better *is* the end of a thing than the beginning thereof: *and* the patient in spirit *is* better than the proud in spirit.'"

*   *   *

In the wake of the plagues came winter, yet the town of New Hope soldiered on even with their stint of bad luck. The farmers had managed a meager second crop late in the season and harvested before the frost could kill it. Even so, there was little food to go around. The season could have been terrible, filled with contempt and distrust due to the accusations and finger-pointing, but it wasn't. The town rallied together, sharing what little they had, helping where they could and being quite neighborly.[85] Even Faithful Goodman and Edith Partridge were downright civil to each other.

Things changed. Not anything drastic. Change is difficult for people, even after triple plagues, but they managed. The change happened deep down and stuck to the soul like lichen on a moist rock. It was because they had a reminder with them, one that played with little husk dolls and had a half-feral cat follow her around. One that let the youngest of children tag along and feel special, one that never made eye-contact with her lively green eyes behind a curtain of straight hair, and always had a scripture on the tip of her tongue.

It would've rounded things out to report that

---

[85] At least more neighborly than normal. In all cases, one is a higher number than zero.

Reverend Michael changed his ways. Unfortunately, change came as easily to the witch-hunter as flying came to fish that were tied to rocks. After New Hope, he continued down the coast looking for witches, perhaps with a little less enthusiasm. He spread the word around that New Hope was a waist-deep cesspool of witches, which did him as much harm as good. Nobody wanted to hire a witch-hunter who entered a perfectly normal town and fled what he could only gracefully describe as "a hole into Hell."

The rumors did deter the usual inflow of travelers, but the gossip eventually faded. Coming full circle, as the story began in rumor, thus it ended. How much grief could have been saved if word-of-mouth had been left well enough alone? What could have been spared? Then again, what wisdom would have been lost? What moral left unlearned? If asked, the people of New Hope would say they were glad for the lesson, for becoming a town full of witches.

After all, they were witches in name only.

Notes

Trial in Name Only is a fictional story, based—sometimes loosely—off of the many witch trials that happened in pre-Revolution America and Europe, one of the most famous being those in Salem, Massachusetts. New Hope and the citizens living there are completely fictional, but Reverend Michael's interrogation methods as well as his skewed sense of justice are based off of historical facts, events and actual witch-hunters—sometimes called witch-finders.

While the dark humor of this tale make light of a horrible event, the truth didn't stray far away. Thousands of people had been accused of performing witch-craft, associating with spirits and devils, and afflicting others; most of whom were tortured and imprisoned solely on baseless evidence such as birthmarks or moles on their bodies, not going to church, or even having an animal—a witch's familiar—touch them during their interrogation. Hundreds were hung (in America and Britain) or burned (throughout Europe).

A majority of those whom were targeted were the elderly, the poor, and those with physical and mental handicaps. A vast majority of the accused were women; it was "common knowledge" back then that women were weaker physically, mentally and spiritually so they were susceptible to evil influences. Children were also accused, the youngest on record was four years old.

The Spanish Inquisition began hunting witches around the fifteenth century. The story of New Hope takes place in the late 1600s a few years before the infamous Salem witch trials, which happened during 1692-93. The last witch arrested for practicing witchcraft happened during World War II in Britain.

If you are interested in more information about these historical witch hunts or read fictional stories that take place in this time frame, please visit your local or school library and talk to the librarian. These wonderful men and women have a sort of magic of their own, but, please, refrain from calling them witches.

No cats or witches were harmed in the making of this book. Feelings on the other hand…

Acknowledgements

First, I'd like to thank the wonderful beta readers on Scribophile and LDS Beta Readers for taking the time and giving me enough feedback to polish this story, especially those who laughed at my gallows humor.

A big thank you to my family who tolerated my absence while churning out this novella in less than a year. Thank you, Tom, for reading it and knowing exactly which word I needed. Thank you, Blain, for all the big hugs when I needed them. Thank you, Lochlan, for distracting me from my work; I probably needed the break anyway.

Thank you Millie for reading this story, even though it isn't your favorite, and yes, *Dragon Treasure* will be the next one.

A shout-out to the special few who watch me on social media and cheer me on whenever I make an update. You are small in number, but large in spirit.

I especially want to thank all the men and women who have formed, organized and run the writing convention LTUE. I have learned so much from the dozens of panels I have attended, and I wish I had the time and the memory to name each and every speaker and author that gave me good advice. You know who you are.

A final thank you to my Heavenly Father. I was born to tell stories, and I am thankful that I have been led down a path that made it possible.

About the Author

Els is a stay-at-home mom, which allows her to do two awesome things at once: raise her two beautiful boys and live her dream as a writer. She is the author of the novel *Thrice-Cursed, Thrice-Blessed*, the novella *Trial in Name Only*, and the co-creator of the short comic "Lenses." Paired with her talented friend, Heather England, they created Psuedo-Sisters, a comic studio where they collaborate on the project *Bittersweet* and future project *Lilies and Daggers*.

Els has a Bachelor's degree from Utah State University in English. She lives in Tooele, Utah with her amazing husband, two sons, and their two dopey dogs, Zorra and Ursa Minor. She enjoys reading fantasies, mysteries and anything by Brandon Sanderson. Her favorite comics are *Girl Genius, Calvin and Hobbes*, and anything with Batman.

Els Curtis would love to hear from her readers. Please write or visit her at either:

ELSCurtis@yahoo.com

www.facebook.com/Curtis.Els

book-hoarder-dragon.tumblr.com